DREAM NEXUS

DREAM NEXUS

Wenonah Lyon

Dream Nexus
Copyright © 2021 Wenonah Lyon

Content Editor: Kerstin Sstokes
Copy Editor: Kirsten Staller
Cover Design: Kristi King-Morgan
Assistant Editor: Amanda Clarke
Editor-in-Chief: Kristi King-Morgan
Formatting: Kristi King-Morgan

ISBN: 9798480539080

www.dreamingbigpublications.com

To my niece, Jean Marie

Chapter One

"The shadow behind the door is my coat, hanging on the hook, nothing from The Dream," Jean Marie whispered to herself. "Just my coat. The junk on the floor is just stuff I left on the floor, not part of The Dream."

She looked at the clock on her bedside table. It was ten minutes until three, the same time she woke up last night, and the night before, and the night before that. Yesterday, she had tried telling her mother about The Dream.

"If you can't remember what you dreamed," her mother said, "how do you know you're dreaming the same thing every night?"

She knew it was the same dream.

Her eyes adjusted to the moonlight. The coat was just a coat and her jeans lying on the floor were just a pair of dirty blue jeans. The cat mewed, complaining, and leaped off the bed, standing in front of the bedroom door.

"Hush," Jean Marie whispered. "You don't want to wake up Mom."

She got up and let the cat out of the room. The hall was dark, but beyond it, the living room was shadowy moon-lit gray.

Jean Marie went down the hall, through the living room, and into the kitchen. She opened the refrigerator door and took out a Coke. She punched in the security code beside the back door and the red light from the burglar alarm stopped blinking.

Stepping from the air-conditioned kitchen into the heat of Texas in August reminded Jean Marie of something from The Dream. She had been hot, much hotter than just coming outside in the summer. She sat down at the patio table. Memories were just beyond recollection, like a name that pops up when you stop thinking about it.

"If you can't sleep, drinking something with caffeine in it won't help," her mother said from the door.

"I don't want to sleep," Jean Marie said.

"Bad dreams again?" her mother asked. Her mother sat down beside her.

Jean Marie didn't answer. *I almost remembered*, she thought resentfully. After a minute, she said, "It's the same dream. I don't remember what happened, but I wake up feeling the same way."

"What do you feel?"

"Hot, I hurt all over, and I'm afraid." She wasn't just afraid, although that was important. "I'm angry, too."

She rolled the cold Coke against her forehead and remembered something from The Dream. "I was hot, very hot all over, and someone put something cold on my forehead and I felt better. I went to sleep." She shivered suddenly. "I remember something else. Somebody wrapping me up, like a mummy, in something like a blanket. Strips of a blanket, wet and hot. Almost hot enough to blister."

***

The cranking of the machine being wheeled into the room woke Jeannette up. The lights in the ward turned on. Jeannette looked at the machine standing at the end of the room and watched the whoosh of flames as the nurse lit the gas jets under it. It was like a washing machine, one of the new, expensive kind. The body was round, a big white enameled belly full of water. There was a wringer on top, like an arm that extended above the belly, where the nurse wrung out the hot strips of wool.

6

First, the nurse wrapped her legs in the wet hot wool. Then, she was left to cook awhile. Finally, the nurse stretched her legs, pulled them straight. She wasn't sure which hurt the most.

"It's for your own good, you know," Stephen said.

Jeannette looked at the boy lying in the bed next to hers.

"You want to be able to walk again? Well, this helps."

"You say that every morning," Jeanette said, "and it hasn't done any good yet. It hurts."

"Sister Kenny said, 'First I hurt you, then it's better.' Trust me."

"I don't believe it."

"You don't want to believe it," Stephen said. "You want to lie there feeling sorry for yourself."

The three-year-old at the end of the row of hospital beds had started to whimper when the machine came onto the ward. He cried louder as the nurse approached him.

"Please," he whimpered.

"The baby has an excuse," Stephen said. "It's a baby. But you're thirteen years old, old enough to put up with something for your own good."

Everyone on the ward was awake now.

Stoically, the machine moved on, slowly advancing between the rows of beds. The baby was quiet. *The nurse must be finished*, Jeannette thought. *Got its bottle now. The baby's going to learn, learn that it doesn't matter how much you cry, it doesn't make any difference.*

There were six beds on each side. Some of them were empty. *Nine people in the room, and my bed's at the end of the line.* She had over an hour to lie and wait for the machine to reach her. She wished they would start at her end.

"This and all the exercises you do, they make a difference. Don't you want out? The doctor thinks I'll be able to go back to school in another couple of months."

"You think they're going to take a cripple?"

"If I can get around with crutches, the Headmaster says he'll hold my place. They're sharing with another school, a big old place in the country. My mates wrote and said not to worry, they'd kick me up the stairs and throw me back down."

"'Mates?' 'Mates?' I thought posh schoolboys had 'chums'."

"I don't know any more about posh schoolboys than you do. Stop trying to take the mickey, Jeannette. I go to the Goldsmiths Boys Academy, not Eton. The school is restricted to boys from the East End. It may be a private school, but it's not for toffs. Half the boys there have scholarships."

Jeannette listened to the machine drawing closer. Matron was wrapping Kevin's legs, and the nurse was beginning to stretch the arms and legs of those at the beginning of the line. Stephen would be wrapped next.

"I'd miss London."

"You don't see a lot of London in here, do you?"

Matron wrapped you up and left you. Left you to cook. Then the nurse came along and did the stretching exercises. Except for the baby. Matron cuddled the baby while he cooked, stretched his little legs, then gave him a bottle and a cuddle. *It hurts me as much as it hurts that old baby.* Stephen was talking to her. He repeated his question.

"Where do you go to school?"

"Don't. After me Nan died, I lived with me Uncle and Auntie. I was ten, they said I could read and figure and that was all I needed to know. I stayed home to take care of the little 'uns."

"There's something else," Stephen said. She heard him sigh. "I want my pencil back."

"I don't know anything about your pencil," Jeannette said.

8

"Yes, you do. I left it on the table between us, and it's gone."

"Must have rolled off. Get the orderly to look under the bed. Or maybe the orderly took it."

"Jeannette, you took it. You're like a little magpie, taking everything. I don't usually care, but this is different, and I want it back. The pencil is special."

Jeannette knew it was special. It was silver, real silver, soft and glowing, a mechanical pencil, with lead inside the pencil and you turned the top to push out the lead. It had Stephen's initials engraved on it. It was shiny and beautiful.

"I don't have your stupid pencil."

"You do. My brother gave it to me before he was sent to France so I could write to him. If you don't give it back, I'll tell Matron you took it. And I'll ask for my bed to be moved."

Jeannette hesitated. Stephen was generous. His father brought him fruit and candy and he shared. His father had brought him a little radio that sat on the table between her bed and his. Stephen listened to the news about the war, which she thought was boring, but he also listened to music or plays, which she enjoyed. She didn't want him to shift to another place on the ward.

She slipped her hand under the mattress and felt the slim pencil. She took it out and handed it to him across the gap between the beds.

"I didn't steal it," she whispered, "I just borrowed it."

He took his pencil.

"Aren't you going to say thank you?" Jeannette asked. Stephen ignored her.

Stupid boy, Jeannette thought. *I only borrowed it.* She wished now she'd thrown it away, slipped it into the wastebasket next to the bed. That would have shown him.

A whimper almost escaped her. The machine was getting closer. She tried to ignore it and thought about The Dream. She would sleep all the time if she could.

There was a girl in The Dream, the same age as her, almost the same name as her. But the girl was tall and slim and pretty, with long dark hair. She whirled and spun around. She took dancing lessons.

Jeannette had always wanted to take dancing lessons.

In the dream, the girl lived in a big house with a big garden, and had a dog and cat. It was not like any house Jeannette had ever seen. It was always cool, no matter how hot it was outside. The house had two bathrooms, both inside, and three bedrooms, with only two people living in the house. *Nicer than Stephen's house,* she thought. A whole room, not being used. Just full of boxes. There was still another room, just for the girl's mother's motor car.

The other person in the dream was the girl's mother. She reminded Jeannette of her Nan, but if she'd ever spoken to her grandmother the way that girl talked to her mother, she'd have gotten a good smack and deserved it. Sometimes, when she was awake, she pretended she and her Nan lived in the house with the dog and cat.

The dream house had no stairs, and her Nan could have gotten around it with no wheezing. Up and down and up and down the stairs, her Nan used to wheeze, sit down, and rest on the landing sometimes. None of that in the dream house. There was no water to carry, either. Water came into the house, like at her uncle's. It was better than her uncle's. Water sprayed on you, like standing out in the rain, only the water was hot.

We would have lodgers in all those extra rooms, Jeannette thought, *and Nan wouldn't have gone out charring.* It was warm in the winter and cool in the summer and in that house, her grandmother would have lived forever.

She was wrapped, cooked, and it was finally over.

10

"I wish Dr. Baron was here," she said. Dr. Baron wrapped and cooked her, but she told her stories, made jokes, and asked riddles.

Jeannette remembered one of the riddles. What's the difference between the Prince of Wales and a bald man? One is the heir apparent, the other has no hair apparent. She didn't know what some of the words meant, but Dr. Baron had explained and didn't make her feel stupid for not knowing.

"Everybody wishes Dr. Baron was here," Stephen said. "But there was a fire, and she's helping there."

It was late, she was sleepy. Stephen was sleepy. Then somebody walked in.

"Dr. Baron! Are you back?"

"No." she said. "Just had to drop in on my way home to see some of my favourite people."

"We miss you," Stephen said, "but you look exhausted, like you ought to get some sleep."

"I had to stop by to pick up some medicine, painkiller. Burns are horribly painful. Plus, the Chaplain took up a collection, called some people he knew, and got donations. People can't work. They still have to eat, so I'll be distributing that as well."

After she left, Jeannette was worried. There were gangs, with a criminal boss, that ran the drug trade. Another gang, with a boss, that controlled gambling. There were other people, like her uncle, that took advantage, working down on the docks, maybe let a crate fall, then share out what was in it. Not really stealing, just giving themselves a bit of the wages they should have got.

But even real criminals would leave the doctor alone. She helped everybody, no matter who. Dr. Baron had her free clinic, and if a criminal showed up with a slashed arm or a gunshot wound, she patched him up.

Still, there were people, just out there that might be lured by money and drugs both. Druggies, for one. You can never trust a druggie. There were others, just plain evil. She thought of her uncle and shivered.

Chapter Two

Jean Marie stood in line, waiting to pay for her lunch. She looked over the crowded cafeteria. Sophie was already in her seat, peanut butter sandwich in hand. She'd had a peanut butter sandwich for lunch for years. *Chicken nuggets and french fries, same school lunch I've had every day for years, too. Same food, same seats in the cafeteria, everybody always in the same seats. Nothing makes people madder than to have somebody take their seat,* Jean Marie thought. She and Sophie sat at the end of the table nearest the door, with half a dozen seats around them empty. The geeks in the chess club sat at the end of their table.

One of them had asked her to the school dance at Thanksgiving, still two months away. She'd said no. He'd turned red and walked back to his end of the table.

Sophie said, "You could have been more gracious."

"I don't do 'gracious'."

"You don't do 'polite' or 'kind', either."

So then Jean Marie had stalked to the end of the table and told the boy it was nothing personal. Her mother didn't let her go places with boys. She came back to Sophie and said, "Satisfied?"

"Good. Now he won't feel like a fool."

"I told a lie. I don't like telling lies. I don't tell lies, usually."

"No, you don't," Sophie said. "But this isn't a real lie. It's a face-saving fiction, done in charity towards others."

Sophie had probably been right, though. The boys at the end of the table were not pushy, but friendly. She thought one of them liked Sophie. He asked her to join the chess club, but she didn't have time. Jean Marie suspected the boy would ask Sophie to the dance, and funny Sophie, that had never been to a school dance, would probably accept. *If she has the clothes. Soph doesn't do a lot of things because she doesn't have the clothes.*

Jean Marie paid for her food and went to her table.

"You're late," Sophie said.

"Computer Science was fun today and I messed around until the next class came in."

"What did you do?"

"Played around with Google. We had to find out how to feed a parrot, what kind of cage it needed, bird diseases. I'd love to have a parrot. In the last ten minutes, Mrs. Carter had us put our names into Google. She says we leave electronic footprints. Most of us came up, usually for dumb things, like finding an announcement of your birth in the paper."

"Cool."

"Mine was better than that. Before we moved to Houston, the Dallas Ballet put on some performances of *The Nutcracker*. I was nine and got chosen to be Clara. I got reviewed in the paper. Good review. Plus, my old ballet teacher has a website, and I'm mentioned there."

"Bringing glory to your teacher's school."

"Right. Have you Googled yourself?"

"Never done anything much. Come on, let's go outside."

"So, you don't think you'd find anything?"

Sophie hesitated.

"Don't tell me," Jean Marie said. "You were an ax-murderer. Sophie Wilmslow took an ax, gave her mother forty whacks. You got off with a really good lawyer."

Sophie laughed. "Not really."

"What would I get if I Googled 'Sophie Wilmslow'?"

"Nothing. But if you typed in 'Kylie Jones', something would come up. No big deal." Jean Marie waited for Sophie to continue.

Why did people change their names? Hiding out from Sophie's father? A witness protection program?

"I came first in San Antonio in the Texas State Spelling Bee for the under-tens," Sophie said. "I messed up when I went to State, though. I missed a really easy word that I should have known."

"A creature of mystery, Ms. Sophia with two names."

"Not much mystery. My mother's second husband adopted me, so I got his last name. I told them I wanted to change my first name as well and they said all right."

"Why 'Sophia'? Much better than 'Kylie', I admit."

"'Sophia' for wisdom. You want to be a prima ballerina. I want to be wise."

"You're already smarter than God."

Sophie didn't laugh. "I'm not talking about learning things. I like that, but being wise is different."

"So, what is wisdom?"

"That's why I like learning things. I'll find out."

The bell rang then. Time for history. Sophie and Jean Marie were in the same history class and the advanced English class. Since Sophie took advanced math and Jean Marie was in the mainstream math class, the rest of their schedules were different. They walked to the classroom.

"Do you still see your adopted father?"

"Nope. When they got divorced, he said he still wanted to see me. My mom said he could see me if he paid child support. He said he'd help out, but wouldn't pay for a kid that wasn't his and my mom wouldn't spend the money on me anyway. He usually remembers my birthday. He gave me my computer when I was nine. Last year, he sent a 50-dollar gift certificate to the bookstore. My mom was furious. She said I needed a new coat, not books."

"He sounds like a nice man."

"He is. But that's the way things go. I'm going to visit him when I'm a grown-up."

They sat down in their seats and saw the three questions written on the board. *Oh no, not a pop test.* Jean Marie, and most of the class, groaned. She hadn't looked at her history assignments for a week. You couldn't put off math, but you could always catch up on history.

"Put your books away and take out a sheet of paper," Mrs. Duncan said. "Answer the questions on the board."

The first question asked what happened on September 1, 1941. The second asked what 'The Phoney War' was. The third was another stupid date, September 3, 1941.

Jean Marie wrote, *September 1, 1941. Britain and France declared war on Germany.*

Well, she thought, *we're studying World War II, that's a good guess. But it's wrong. It's absolutely wrong.* She scribbled it out and wrote, *Germany invaded Poland.*

The Phoney War. Jean Marie wrote, *After war was declared, nothing happened between September 3, 1939, and May 1940. People expected to be bombed and children were sent from the cities to the country.*

Again, Jean Marie was sure of her answer. *I suppose I saw it on the History Channel or some PBS special,* she thought.

Finally, September 3, 1941. *England and France declared war on Germany.*

I know these answers, I'm not guessing. It's not any after school special on public television. I dreamed about this. She remembered a girl and boy looking at newspapers. The girl said it didn't matter. Poland was a long way away. The boy said don't be stupid. France and England signed a pact and said they'd protect Poland if anybody attacked her.

They're not just dreams. Jean Marie felt afraid. *Now I can remember them. It's like they've all come back to me. I know what The Dreams are about.*

They passed their answers to the front of the room and Mrs. Duncan collected them. She asked something about Chamberlain and peace in our time. Sophie was going on about not trusting dictators.

Jean Marie heard another voice, an old man, and for just a minute she had an image in her mind of a man, a woman, and a young man sitting by the bed of the boy in the hospital. She was seeing it, she realized, through the girl's eyes. The old man was talking.

"Spaceship to Earth, spaceship to Earth, calling Jean Marie, hello?"

The class laughed.

"Jean Marie, now we have your attention, what can we learn from Chamberlain's negotiations with Hitler?"

"I don't think Chamberlain exactly trusted Hitler…it wasn't that simple." Jean Marie said slowly. She tried to remember what the old man had said. "People remembered World War I and all the killing. France lost a whole generation of young men. War had to be the last option and people had to see it was the last option or they wouldn't accept it. Everybody, not just Chamberlain, wanted to avoid war. So, he played for time. 'Peace in our time,' he said. Chamberlain hoped Hitler would look East, and Stalin and Hitler would destroy each other. Then the Hitler-Stalin Non-Aggression Pact…"

Jean Marie put together information from the dates. "Germany and the Soviet Union pact August 23, 1939, Poland was invaded on September 1, 1939, war declared September 3, 1939."

The old man had cried when he ticked the three dates off, one by one, on his fingers.

After class, Jean Marie walked to her locker with Sophie and Dawn.

"That stuff you said, a lot of it wasn't in the book," Sophie said.

"I must have seen a movie about it or something."

"Now that would be a great way to learn history. Just watch the movie," Dawn said.

Jean Marie laughed and gave her a shove. She said, "A movie with dates and treaties? I can just see you watching that, Dawn."

"Well, it's better than reading a boring book."

Dawn put her books in her locker and left to join her friends.

Jean Marie said, "Soph, I don't know how I knew what I said in class. Well, I do, I dreamed it, but I don't know how I knew about it to dream it."

"A movie, like you said. There're a lot of movies about the beginning of the Second World War. Did you ever see Casablanca?"

"Yeah," Jean Marie said. "It was a good movie, but she should have gone off with what's his name, Bogart, at the end. But Soph, there was nothing like that in the movie."

"Some other book, movie or TV show, probably something on the History Channel you didn't pay much attention to, covered the information. Your unconscious stored it and you remembered the information without knowing how you knew it. That's the most logical explanation."

"That may be logical, but it's not what I remember. I remember The Dream." Jean Marie had a clear picture of the old man and his fingers, ticking things off. "Can you think of an illogical explanation?"

"Sure. Time travel, alternate universes, reincarnation. If you read science fiction, you could think of all kinds of explanations. But it's fiction, not science. Remember Sherlock Holmes? When you have eliminated the impossible, whatever remains, however improbable, must be the truth. It may be improbable that you read a book or saw a documentary, but it's the least improbable explanation. Anything else is California psychobabble."

"Well, I say it's a dream, and if you're not going to listen to what I say, I might as well not talk to you."

"Oh, come on, J.M.," Sophie said. "Tell me something that doesn't have a natural explanation and I'll consider the supernatural. So far, everything you've talked about is either common knowledge or you can't check it. Until then, let's not fight about it."

"I've got to catch my bus," Jean Marie said. "And yours looks like it's getting ready to go. See you tomorrow."

Jean Marie boarded the school bus. All the seats were taken. It was hot and noisy. When the bus driver started the engine, a blast of hot air came from the air conditioner. *It won't cool off before I get home*, Jean Marie thought. *I shouldn't have wasted time arguing with Sophie. Sometimes, she's is a very irritating best friend.*

She remembered the first time she'd met Sophie. She had just moved to Houston and started fifth grade. Soph still looked the same, a fat little kid they used to call 'short and wide' or 'two by four'. She wore her hair in high pigtails, over her ears. Her hand was always the first up. The rest of the class acted like Sophie didn't exist, but Jean Marie was interested in her.

On the second or third day, Jean Marie noticed Sophie sitting on the wall reading a book at recess. She'd stood, watching her. Then Sophie looked up and smiled. While she was walking toward Sophie, Cecilia Rogers came up to Sophie and put out her hand. Sophie reached in her pocket and gave her something. Cecilia waited for Jean Marie and Sophie shook her head slightly, trying to keep Jean Marie from coming over.

Jean Marie kept walking.

When she got to the two girls, Cecilia said, "There's a tax on new students. Give me a quarter."

"No way," Jean Marie said.

"Then I'll beat you up."

"Don't be silly. I'll tell a teacher."

Cecilia was surprised, but she walked away.

"Why don't you just tell her to get lost?" Jean Marie had asked Sophie. "Or tell a teacher. Teachers aren't going to let somebody steal your money or beat you up. Cecilia knows that. She just walked off. I heard she's been suspended once and the next time she gets expelled."

"Our situations are different. She rides my school bus and she lives in the trailer park where I live. She has opportunities to thump me away from school. I'm a pragmatist. It's easier to give her the money."

"What's a pragmatist?"

"Somebody that does what's reasonable and sensible in a situation. What's practical for you may not be what's practical for me."

Jean Marie said, "You could take judo. Then you could beat her up."

"I don't think I'd be very good at judo. You look athletic. Do you know judo?"

"No. I take ballet. You get as many muscles dancing as you do playing football or basketball."

"You're not like anybody else in the class."

"Neither are you."

They had become best friends.

***

Stephen and Jeannette had been shifted from the hospital ward to a small private room. Most of the children had been sent home or to hospitals outside London during the Phoney War. They kept Stephen because his physical therapy was going well. They thought he could join his school in Surrey in another month. They kept her because they couldn't find her uncle to sign the papers.

Instead, their ward was full of wounded soldiers. The war had taken over the rest of the world, why not their ward?

Stephen's father said most of the trains from Dover were bringing wounded soldiers up to the London hospitals. They took them off the boats and brought the worst to hospitals near Dover. The rest of the wounded came on trains to London.

When the first trains pulled into Victoria Station, Stephen's father went to see if he could find his son. He said it was a madhouse, train after train pulling in. The police wouldn't let anybody in.

There wasn't any word about Stephen's older brother. The nurses promised to tell Stephen if he were brought to their hospital.

The summer she was eight, before her Nan died, she and her Nan had gone hop-picking in Kent, in Canterbury, near Dover. Her Nan called it a working holiday. The children her age had watched the little 'uns while the grown-ups picked. Up and down the rows, men cut the long strings of hops growing over the wooden frames while women gathered them and threw them into the back of the trailer. Older women, like her Nan, pulled the pale green hops off the stems and put them in boxes. The children had been told to look sharpish, and her uncle had tapped the side of his nose.

They'd looked sharpish, and brought back potatoes from the fields, apples from the orchard. At night, they roasted them in the fire where they camped. All the London people were from the East End like she was. They camped together. Sometimes they bought sausages and cooked them over the fire. They sang songs and drank beer and cider. It had been a good, proper holiday.

"Stephen," Jeannette said, "you know how hops grow?"

"On trees? Bushes, like gooseberries?" he said.

"On vines, like grapes. Like very light green grapes the same color as their leaves." Jeannette was pleased she knew something Stephen didn't.

"So what?"

"You got to have hops to make beer. Hops grow in Kent. Think there'll be a shortage of beer? When the Nazis start bombing Kent?"

"For heaven's sake, Jeannette, who cares if there's a shortage of beer? Besides, why should the Germans waste bombs on Kent? It's just a bunch of farms. Now be quiet and let me tune the radio. It's almost time for the nine o'clock news."

Stephen fiddled with his small radio, and the nurse came into the room to listen to it.

I don't know why we want to listen, Jeannette thought, *it's only more bad news. Blitzkrieg, the lightning war. Blitzkrieg this and Blitzkrieg that…Holland and Belgium fell. And it was like being struck by lightning. Flash! Norway and Denmark gone.* It seemed like every day another country fell. Then, the Panzer divisions divided the British and French Armies in Northern France.

Her cousin, Paul, had been mad for motor cars. He said they'd take over the country someday. Well, Germany's motorized army was taking over a bunch of countries.

Jeannette remembered how Stephen had looked when they learned that the British Expeditionary Force was in retreat. His father brought him a map, and every day more chunks of France were gone. Yesterday, the Germans took Boulogne.

Tonight, they learned Calais had been occupied. After the radio was turned off, Jeannette said, hesitantly, "Calais…that's the nearest French port to Dover. That's where they were evacuating the troops, wasn't it?"

"Yes, you little nitwit. Calais and Boulogne are now both under Nazi occupation."

Matron said, "Stephen…"

Jeannette said, "There's other ports, Stephen. There're lots of towns along the coast."

The map of France was dotted with little towns right on the channel.

"Miss Cockney Sparrow, chirp, chirp, chirp. Yes, there are other towns, nice shallow water resorts where people swim or you can fish or put out a dinghy. But not deepwater ports, with piers where the Navy can dock. Dunkirk is the only port left that can handle the battleships and the big passenger ferries picking up soldiers."

"Enough," the nurse said. "It's not over yet. Stephen, you're feverish. You need something to help you sleep."

Jeannette lay awake, listening to Stephen snore. She wasn't angry. If yelling at her and calling her names made him feel better, let him do it.

There was no moonlight; blackout drapes shut light out and shut light in. There was a dim light at the end of the hall, where the night nurse was sitting, and Jeannette could see the Evil Machine in the corner. It was still fired up three times a day and the hot wool strips wrapped around her legs. At least it was just her legs, not her whole self. Evil Machines. Who could imagine a washing machine and a motor car could make her hurt like this?

She reached over and took the newspaper the nurse brought Stephen. She tore a strip of newspaper off, chewed it, and took it out of her mouth. A very good spitball, nice and juicy. It might even stick to the Evil Machine.

She aimed and threw. Gotcha!

Chapter Three

When Jean Marie got home, she opened the front door and saw no blinking light. She'd forgotten to set the burglar alarm when she left for school. *No big deal*, she thought, *there's nothing to steal but the TV.* Muffin jumped on her, then rushed to the back door., waiting to go outside. She let him out.

She got a Coke and some potato chips from the kitchen, and sat down on the floor, leaning back against the sofa. She picked up the telephone and called Sophie.

"J. M.?" Sophie said.

"Yup."

Jean Marie picked up the remote control and clicked on the television.

"Good show today?" Jean Marie asked.

"You wouldn't believe these freaks today," Sophie said.

Jean Marie heard the dog scratching at the back door over the sound of the television crowd: "Jeree, Jeree, Jeree…"

"Got to let the dog in, Soph…there…he's in. How do you think people lived in Texas before air conditioning?"

"Uncomfortably."

Jean Marie stretched out on the floor again, the telephone cradled against her ear. "I don't believe these people are for real. Nobody would go on national TV and tell that kind of stuff."

"But can there be that many big-haired trailer trash actresses in the world?" Sophie imitated a guest on the show, "My bleep bleep bleep boyfriend left me for my bleep grandmother…now he's bleeping moved in with my aunt…"

Jean Marie lowered her voice and pretended to be the boyfriend, "Well, Jeree, a man's got to look out for hisself…I thought the old lady had a bigger pension. I don't know what the bleeping government is comin' to, expecting a little old lady to live on bleeping cat food."

The girls laughed.

"My mom called your mom today," Sophie said. "She asked if I could sleepover this weekend. She's got a heavy date, going to Mexico for the weekend."

"Who with?"

"Some pig. My mother has no judgment where men are concerned. This one is low-life pond scum even by her standards. My poor mother," Sophie continued. "I think she suffers from low self-esteem."

"I think you've been watching too much *Oprah* and *Jeree.*"

"You can't watch too much *Oprah* and *Jeree.* Except now. I better hang up. I've got to get the breakfast dishes washed and supper cooked before Mom gets home," Sophie said.

"What are you fixing?"

"Hamburger, baked potato, a nice salad. Maybe I'll boil some corn."

"Yuck. Hamburger's okay, but the rest is yuck."

"You're a dedicated carnivore," Sophie said. "You're going to die of some vitamin deficiency if you don't eat more vegetables."

"I'll take a pill. I've got to practice. See you in school tomorrow."

Jean Marie hung up the phone and stood behind the sofa in the middle of the room. Slowly, she did her warm-up exercises, stretching, concentrating on the feel of the muscles in her arms and legs. As she continued, she felt the muscles in her back and shoulders relax. Then she put her hand on the back of the sofa and began her ballet exercises.

Her concentration was broken when she heard her mother open the front door. She glanced at the clock. She'd been practicing almost an hour.

"Hi, sweetie. I'm home," her mother said as she came into the room. "Guess who called me today?"

"Sophie's mom. Let me do my winding down exercises," Jean Marie said.

"Go ahead, I'll talk." Her mother went into the kitchen and got a glass of orange juice. "I suppose Sophie told you she'd be coming over on Friday."

"Uggg," Jean Marie grunted.

"That wasn't the only call I got today," her mother said. "Mrs. Duncan called."

"Oh?" Jean Marie said warily. She stood up. "I'm sweating like a pig. I'm going to take a shower."

"You don't have to worry, nothing bad. She said she'd called me often enough because she was concerned,"

"Concerned," Jean Marie said, rolling her eyes.

"Yes, concerned. She is a concerned and good teacher. And a very fair teacher. She said she'd complained about you often enough so she thought she should call to tell me how well you were doing. She said you were well-prepared and had been reading extra material. She was delighted with your comments today. She said you had a real feeling for history, the past, and a sensitivity and understanding unusual in someone your age."

"Whatever," Jean Marie muttered.

"Tell you what, Friday night, we'll go to a nice restaurant, you and me and Sophie, and have a girl's night out."

"Whatever…" Jean Marie said again.

After dinner, Jean Marie sat staring at her math book. She'd tried to avoid thinking about what happened in class. Whatever Sophie said, there wasn't an explanation.

There was a boy, there was a girl, they were in a hospital. World War II was going on.

In The Dream, she was the girl. The girl thought a lot of strange things. She thought if she drank milk and ate fish at the same time, she'd get cancer. She really thought that, she wasn't just trying to get out of drinking milk.

I know her name, Jean Marie thought. *I know her name is Jeannette Bagg.* Jean Marie realized she knew much more about Jeannette than her name. *I know everything about Jeannette. I know her as well as I know myself. I don't know the others, Stephen, the hospital people, Stephen's father. I only know as much about them as Jeannette does. Sophie thinks I want to prove Jeannette is real. She's wrong. I want Sophie to convince me that it's not true, that I am not watching a girl and a boy in London during the war, that the dreams are pieces of books and movies and TV shows. Most of all, I want her to convince me that Jeannette and I are different people, that I'm not Jeannette, and that Jeannette isn't some kind of witch that's sneaked into my head.* She shivered, afraid. *I hate her. I hate Jeannette. She's a nasty, sly, stupid girl, she lies and steals and she's not me. She's selfish and she hates it when anything good happens to somebody else. She's not me. I'm not her. I don't want her life, and I'm not going to let her steal mine.*

***

"Little boats, little boats," Stephen cried out. "Who would have thought it? Little boats, not big boats. Little boats picking up French and English all up and down the coast, taking them to the big boats."

Jeannette looked at the newspapers scattered over Stephen's bed. His father had bought them all. They read the headlines:

27

"Saved"

"Disaster Turned To Triumph"

"Rescued From The Jaws Of Death"

Jeannette watched Stephen's father and Matron exchange glances. Stephen's father had fought in the trenches in World War I. Matron had been a nurse over there, in France. They looked grim. Stephen's father shrugged slightly, and Matron shook her head.

"Not too excited, Stephen," she said.

"Who could not be excited?" Stephen asked. "It's like Agincourt or Wellington at the Battle of Trafalgar or Xenophon and the ten thousand!"

Jeannette had no idea who any of those people were. *Stephen might be smart and he might know a lot of things out of books, but sometimes he doesn't notice what's important.* His dad and Matron didn't look happy. *They don't want to discourage him, so they're not saying anything.*

Nobody looking at their faces could think this was any kind of triumph.

"Jeannette, what's wrong with you? Stop being a lump and think about this! It's like Henry the V, and we'll tell our grandchildren about this day…when the flotilla of little ships set sail, men and even women hiding their long hair, dressed in trousers, went to bring the British Expeditionary Force home. Little ships, little boats, sailing boats, ferries, motorboats," he chanted, "and the Gods looked down and the sea was calm and there was even a light mist to confuse the German bombers."

"Enough," Matron said. "You're over-excited, Stephen."

"But it was glorious," Stephen said. "Glorious and brave and it will be a day remembered in history."

"Glorious, yes," Matron said. "But you need to get to sleep."

"Off you go," she said to Stephen's father. "Stephen and Jeannette, would you like a cup of warm milk to help you sleep?"

"No, Matron," they both said.

Jeannette lay awake, watching Matron at her desk outside the room, watching the clock that hung on the wall. At 4 a.m., Matron came in to check on her.

"You're awake?" Matron whispered. "Pain? Do you want something to help?"

"Matron," Jeannette whispered, "have we lost the war?"

"No," Matron whispered. "We have not lost this war and we are not going to. We evacuated our troops and we'll regroup, that's all. Now, to sleep with you." Matron went back to the hall to her desk.

"What does that mean in ordinary English?" Jeannette whispered.

"It means," Stephen said in an ordinary voice, "that the Germans kicked us out of France and we are totally disorganized."

"But we haven't been beaten yet," Matron called from the hall. "Five hundred thousand troops were brought home on naval ships, cargo ships, channel ferries, and those little boats sailed by brave, ordinary people. It was not a victory, Stephen, but it's not a defeat. Now the pair of you, no talking. Sleep. The Prime Minister is giving a speech tomorrow night. We'll listen to it on Stephen's radio and your father's coming after visiting hours and listening with us. We'll have cocoa and biscuits for a treat and listen to what Churchill has to say."

Jeannette and Stephen were quiet.

Jeannette remembered something the girl in her dream had read, something Prime Minister Churchill said. She shut her eyes, and the page appeared before her: She whispered to Stephen, "We shall go on to the end, we shall fight in France, we shall fight on the seas and oceans, we shall fight with growing confidence and growing strength in the air, we shall defend our island, whatever the cost may be, we shall fight on the beaches, we shall fight on the landing grounds, we shall fight in the fields and in the streets, we shall fight in the hills; we shall never surrender…"

Stephen was looking at her oddly. "You had to hear that. It didn't come out of your head."

"Churchill," Jeannette said, "his speech."

"I haven't heard that speech or read it in the papers," Stephen said. "I'm the one that listens to speeches and reads the papers, not you. He hasn't said that."

"Not yet. He'll give the speech tomorrow night."

The next night, Matron brought in chairs from the hall. She and Stephen's father sat at the ends of the two beds. Stephen tuned the radio, and they heard the announcement from the BBC. Prime Minister Churchill began to talk.

Jeannette heard the words again. She felt proud. The speech ended.

"A good speech," Stephen's father said. "No lies. We're in a bad place, but we'll get out."

After Matron and his father had gone, Stephen said, "How did you know?"

Jeannette felt afraid. Stephen looked angry, and he'd be even angrier when she told him. He wouldn't believe her. She'd told so many lies, he'd think this was just another one.

"I dreamed it," she mumbled.

"Dreamed it?"

"There's this girl…I dream about her sometimes."

"I've read about people who have dental work, fillings, picking up radio broadcasts," Stephen said.

"I got no fillings," Jeanette said. "I've never been to a dentist. Where would we get the money for dentists?"

"You heard it before the broadcast anyway. Mental telepathy, perhaps," Stephen said. "The Prime Minister was writing his speech and you somehow tapped into his thoughts."

"No," Jeannette objected. "I dream about a girl. In the dreams, the girl is learning about our war in school. I liked the dreams at first, when I thought they were just dreams. Now they scare me."

When Stephen didn't answer, Jeannette said, "Stephen? I'm not lying. Really. If I didn't dream it, how would I know it?"

"I believe you," Stephen said. "I'm trying to think of how you dreamed it." After a minute, he said, "Did you dream about who won the war?"

"They haven't got to that part yet."

"I read somewhere that if you gave an infinite number of monkeys an infinite number of typewriters and infinite time, they'd type out all the plays of Shakespeare."

"You're just making fun of me," Jeannette said. "See if I tell you anything."

"How am I making fun of you?"

"You called me a monkey."

"No, I didn't."

"Yes, you did."

"I was just remembering something I read about chance. Well, it was really about infinity, but it was also about probability. Anyway, if monkeys could type Hamlet just by pecking at random typewriter keys, you could come up with part of a speech in a dream. But maybe it's precognition, maybe you're seeing the future. That's much more likely than chance. You're maybe a seeress, not a monkey."

"I know I'm not a monkey. Even you know I'm not a monkey. But what you are saying, really, is that I'm stupid, like a monkey, and if I know anything or do anything it's something even a monkey could do."

"Oh, go to sleep. You are the silliest girl I have ever known."

The room was quiet. Stephen started to snore. *The future,* Jeannette thought. *I hate the future.*

Sometimes, Matron gave her a pencil and a book of games with mazes in it. She would take the pencil and draw a path through the maze. There was always a way through the maze, some path that was not blocked, where she could find her way to the center. The future was a maze with everything blocked. There was nowhere to go and no way out

At first, she'd hated the hospital. Now the worst was over, it was cozy. A very cozy place, with nice food that came regular, and it was warm. Matron was kind. She even liked the tutor helping her with schoolwork. Stephen couldn't understand why she didn't work harder at physical therapy so she could go home.

This is much better than home. Besides, I don't have a home anymore.

Chapter Four

Sophie sprawled on Jean Marie's bed eating chocolate ice cream. Jean Marie sat in front of her computer.

"Doesn't mean a thing," Sophie said. "Jeannette Bagg and Stephen Finkelstein may not live in London today, Jeannette might have changed her name, they'd be very old and might be living with their children or in an old people's home. They may not have a telephone. Or they may have a cell phone instead of a landline, so they wouldn't be in the London telephone book."

"There's an option for changing cities," Jean Marie said.

"It wouldn't mean a thing if you did find the name. Why should the telephone Bagg be your Bagg?"

"What would mean something?"

"Finding a newspaper article saying that Dr. Stephen Finkelstein, despite his handicap from having polio when he was a child, overcame all difficulties to win the Noble Prize in something or other."

"Many are called but few are chosen. There's not a whole lot of Noble Prize winners in the world." Jean Marie looked at her bowl of ice cream. "Yuck. Melted."

The hovering dog looked eager and whined. She put the bowl down on the floor and the dog began licking.

"Jean Marie! Chocolate is poison for dogs. Don't do that."

"I do it all the time. I always share with Muffin. Don't I, Muffin?"

Jean Marie leaned back and looked at her computer screen. "Where are all those electronic footprints they talked about in computer class? Jeannette and Stephen must have little bitty feet. But the hospital…the hospital ought to still be around."

"That's another matter. Not finding the hospital was a blow."

"It's too bad it's not you and Stephen having the dreams. The two of you would have thought of some clever way of figuring this out. Me and Jeannette don't have that kind of mind. All Jeannette thinks about is food, and how much she likes hospital food. That and whining about how other people get more pudding than she does, or how it's not fair she's sick. Did I tell you Stephen called her a monkey?"

"You're too hard on her."

"She's creepy." Jean Marie changed the subject. "Do you know what the Grand National is?"

"Never heard of it."

"It must be some kind of sport thing, like the World Series or the Super Bowl. Stephen thinks maybe Jeannette is telepathic and picked up the speech that way. He doesn't believe she's in touch with the future. He wants Jeannette to ask us to tell him the winner of the Grand National."

Jean Marie went back to Google. "Grand National England" had pages of entries. She opened one. "It's a horse race."

She skimmed through the information on the site. "A race called a steeplechase. The horses don't run around a flat track. They jump over barriers. Here's a picture."

Sophie came over to the screen. "Do we have steeplechase races in this country?"

"Don't know. Don't care. Maybe. It looks like a lot of the horses get killed. Well, not a lot. One every couple of years."

Jean Marie opened a section of the site called "Past Winners." Then she took a felt tip pen and printed a large note on a sheet of paper: "WINNER 1940 GRAND NATIONAL - BOGSCAR. RACE SUSPENDED 1941-1945" and taped it to her wall.

"There," she said. "I don't know when the Grand National was. It might have been before June 1940. They still have the races, and now they're in the spring. It would be real proof if I could give the 1941 results as well but they must have quit holding the races during the war."

"Why did you write it down and put it on the wall?"

"I don't know when Jeannette is going to be watching me. This way, if I'm in my room, she'll see it."

"Clever. Here, give me the paper and pen." Sophie took them and wrote, in large letters, "To Stephen and Jeannette, We are real. Are you? With very highest regards, Sophia Wilmslow, Jean Marie's friend."

"If they haven't had the race yet, Stephen may be satisfied. I'm not," Jean Marie said. "Not finding the hospital bothers me. After we saw the pictures, I remembered National Velvet. It was a movie, and it was about a steeplechase."

"It was a long time ago, sixty-five years."

"Not that long," Jean Marie said. "My grandfather fought in the Second World War. Don't say he could have told me stories and that's another possible explanation. He fought in the Pacific, not Europe. What about you? What did your grandparents do during the war?"

"No idea," Sophie said. "My mother got pregnant with me and they kicked her out. She was sixteen, and I ruined her life. But they won't have me or her in the house. My grandfather's some kind of religious nut."

"You ruined her life? She did something stupid. If anybody ruined her life but her, it was her parents."

Sophie said, "My mom wouldn't agree. She blames both my grandfather and me." Sophie changed the subject. "What's your happiest memory?"

Jean Marie thought about it. "It's hard to decide. Maybe when I graduated from the baby slopes to finally skiing downhill. It was like flying. Or, when I finally got my first pair of toe shoes. I'd wanted them for years, but my teacher kept saying I wasn't ready. Maybe when I was chosen to be Clara in The Nutcracker. There're so many good memories, it's hard to choose the best. What's your best?"

"After the spelling bee, my adopted father took me on one of his trips. He's a truck driver and goes all over the United States. He said when I lost at State that it didn't matter, and I deserved a prize anyway. He was delivering a load to Phoenix and I went with him. After, we went to the Grand Canyon and spent the weekend. I bought a poster. The Grand Canyon goes on and on with the different rock strata, different colors. It's so much more than the picture. That was great. Really great." Sophie yawned. "I'm about to fall asleep. We'll look at our problem again tomorrow. This, Watson, is a three pipe problem."

"What! It's not elementary, Sherlock?"

"Only after you figure it out, Watson. That's when it becomes elementary."

Jean Marie turned out the light. She was almost asleep when Sophie said, "J.M., does your mother have a boyfriend?"

"Sort of," Jean Marie said. "There's this guy she went out with, but his company got rid of a lot of people and he took a job in San Diego."

"Did you like him?"

"He was okay. I was polite, he was polite."

"Have you ever thought of what you'd do if your mom got married?"

"Why should she do that?"

"She might be lonely."

"She's not lonely. She's got me, a sister, parents across town, a dog, a cat, and plenty of friends."

"You won't be around much longer."

"She can get married then."

Jean Marie thought of what Sophie had said. "Do you think your mom is thinking about getting married?"

"She's only known this guy a couple of weeks. She believes in love at first sight and she thinks love means marriage." Sophie yawned. "She will or she won't, and there's not a thing I can do about it."

***

Jean Marie woke up to the smell of bacon. *Saturday,* she thought sleepily. Saturday mornings meant sleeping in and sitting around the kitchen table with a big breakfast. Sunday mornings were different. When she was little, Sunday mornings meant getting up and driving to the newsstand. Her mother bought the New York Times and she got a comic book, usually Little Lulu or Donald Duck. Then they bought a box of freshly fried donuts. At home, she and her mom would crawl into her mom's bed and eat the donuts while they were still warm. Her mother would read the news sections, she'd read the comic.

It had been years since they'd done that.

She heard Sophie's voice in the kitchen and got up.

"How come," she asked her mother, "we don't still get donuts and the Times on Sunday?"

"Too much sugar, too much fat," her mother said. "and I look at the Times online."

"Can we do it tomorrow morning anyway? Since Sophie's here?"

"I suppose so. This morning, bacon and waffles. Are you ready for your first waffle?"

"Mrs. Hastings," Sophie said, "Do they put everything in a newspaper online?"

"Not everything."

"I tried to look at the London Times," Jean Marie said. "You can look at some things from the last seven days free. You have to pay otherwise."

"What were you looking for?" her mother asked.

"I wanted to read about London in 1940."

"There are other websites that have newspaper articles in them," her mother said. "The BBC has a good history section."

"I want to look at things in general, not important events." Jean Marie tried to frame her question. "All those sites are what somebody else thinks is important after the fact."

"In that case, abandon the web and try the library. We've got the complete Times on microfiche. You can come down some time and look at it."

"This morning?"

"Maybe your mother's busy," Sophie said.

"No, I was just going to clean the house. I'd much rather go to the library."

"We're doing my mother a favor, aren't we?"

Her mother laughed. She said, "I don't think I'd call it a favor, but I don't mind. I've got some work I can do in my office. I'll set you up with a microfiche and you can get me when you're finished."

At the university, Mrs. Hastings set them up in a library cubicle in the microfiche section. She had a box labeled 1939 and 1940 full of spools of film. She threaded the first one on the machine and flipped the switch. A light lit up the screen, and she adjusted the machine until the print was readable.

"Cool," Jean Marie said. "It's like a slide projector."

"You turn the crank, here, and the next page comes up," her mother said. "I'll leave you to it. I'll be in my office when you finish."

The girls sat flipping through page after page.

"They still had plays in the West End, even though there were bombs," Sophie said.

Jean Marie saw a picture.

"That's him. Stephen."

There was a picture in the Times with Stephen wearing a hospital gown. A woman in a nurse's uniform stood next to him. The newspaper article reported that Sister Kenny had come from Australia to teach the methods she had devised to use with polio patients. Jean Marie remembered her first dreams, with the hot strips of cloth and the stretching, and how painful the treatment was.

In the article, they found Stephen's name. "Fourteen year old Stephen Finkelstein will be one of the patients to benefit from Sister Kenny's new approach."

"Proof!" Jean Marie said

"Proof." Sophie said. "Proof of something. Now we need to figure out what it's proof of."

***

"I knew Boscar won the Grand National," Jeannette said. "Then they said next year's Grand National is canceled. That's how fortunetellers work. My Nan didn't hold with fortune-tellers. She said it was a waste of money."

"Your Nan was probably right," Stephen said. "It was smart of them to put up a letter to us, in case you weren't dreaming at the right time."

"Sophie wrote you a note. She said they were real and asked if you were."

Stephen grinned and picked up a piece of paper and pencil. He thought a minute and wrote, "Dear Sophie, What's real? I'm sure of me, willing to think you are possible, and suspect that Jeannette is a figment of my imagination. With best regards, Stephen Finkelstein."

"How can we stick it over the bed?" Stephen said.

"Spit wads. We chew up some paper and stick it on the wall."

"That's disgusting." He considered it. "Besides, the paper's too heavy for spit wads to keep it up."

"Give it here."

Jeannette took Stephen's note and cut two slits at the top of the page. She took another piece of paper and cut two strips from it. She threaded the strips through the slits she had made and slipped them over the top rail to her bed. Then she took her pot of glue and glued the ends of the strips.

After a minute, Jeannette asked, "Stephen, Jean Marie said I was creepy. She doesn't like me."

"She doesn't know you. She's probably scared of The Dream."

"I don't like her."

"You don't know her, either. Come on, monkey-punky, your dreams add considerably to life here in the boring old hospital."

Matron came into the room and noticed the note on the top rail of Jeannette's bed.

"What's this?"

Jeannette said, "Stephen wrote it and I put it up. If I'm a figment of his imagination, when his candy and fruit all disappear, he can't complain. Figments of imagination don't creep in the middle of the night and steal your sweets."

Matron laughed. "A very good point, Jeannette. And when imaginary figments have tummy aches in the middle of the night due to their greed, I can just ignore them.

"You two are in a good mood this morning. Stephen, you're going to be in an even better mood. A letter, from your brother."

Stephen opened the letter and read it. "He can't tell me where it is, but I know he's still in Britain. He says it's cold and the people don't speak English. Must be Scotland or Wales. He says he ate a haggis. Must be Scotland."

Matron was amused. "Don't let Sister MacGregor hear you saying the Scottish don't speak English. I've been on holiday in Scotland, and the countryside is beautiful. If your brother likes walking or climbing, he'll enjoy his free time."

Jeannette thought of what she'd heard about Jews. They had special butchers. They didn't eat some things. How could Stephen's brother eat haggis?

She asked, "Stephen, I thought Jewish people had to have special food."

"It depends on how religious you are. My family's not very religious. My father goes to the synagogue at Passover and Yom Kippur. We don't eat pork. But that's about it. What about your family? Are you religious?"

"Christenings, marriages, and funerals. The family likes a good funeral. Me Nan paid tuppence a week to the man for years so she'd have a proper funeral. Every Friday at six o'clock, after tea, he'd come around, knocking on the door."

"Was it a good funeral?" Stephen asked.

"The best funeral our street ever saw. A white, shiny casket lined with pink satin. Me Nan picked it out herself. A big, comfy coffin. A bit too big, actually."

Jeannette giggled. "Thump, thump, thump. It were horrible, horrible, but you had to laugh. Me Uncle Dan always said me Nan liked a bit of a laugh more than anyone, and she was laughing in the coffin herself."

Jeannette paused and continued her story. "We had the laying out in the front room of me Uncle Frank's house. He had the most room. Everybody loved me Nan, and they all wanted to come to view the body: neighbors, relatives, everybody. Uncle Frank had a nice little terraced house, two up, two down. Downstairs, there's the hall, the front room nobody goes into, and the kitchen. The stairs in the hall take you upstairs to two more rooms.

"Me Nan died on a Thursday and me aunts washed the body. That night, the undertaker's men came and set up the coffin on trestles, like a carpenter uses, with a nice pink satin cloth over the trestles that matched the coffin lining.

"The undertaker's men shuffled us all into the kitchen, 'cause it makes people cry to see the coffin come in. All-day Friday, people came in and out of the house, somebody sitting by the coffin at all times. Most people came Friday night, after work. There were flowers everywhere. There was a bunch from the grandchildren, with my name on it. So, we see me Nan, looking peaceful and almost alive, only with more make-up than she usually wore. They paint 'em up like trollops, men and women. Ten o'clock that night, the undertaker's men come and close the coffin, and screwed it down tight.

"Next morning, they come back, this time with the two black horses with black plumes pulling the hearse. Clump, clump, clump down the street, and everybody comes out and stands in front of their house. All the men take their caps off, showing respect. The undertaker's men with their white gloves take us all into the kitchen and close the door.

"We're standing there, nobody saying anything, and we hear this 'thump, thump, thump.'

"Aunt Masie says, 'What's that'

"Uncle Frank says, 'They've turned the coffin up straight to get it out into the hall and me mam is getting shaken around inside, that's what it is.'

"Then we hear bad language from the hall. B this and GD that…and one of the men says, 'It ain't gonna go.'

"Uncle Frank throws open the kitchen door and is going to head-butt whoever is cursing his mother.

"'We ain't cursing your mam,' the man says, 'we're cursing the hall and the door. The top of the door frame is blocking the coffin when we tilt it to get it out.'

"'How'd you get it in in the first place?' Uncle Frank asks.

"'We tilted the coffin through the sitting room door with the lid off and got it in. Now the lid's screwed down and it won't go.'

"'So unscrew the lid, you lazy buggers, and screw it up after.'

"'Can't do that, mate. It's been overnight, long enough there'd be a bit of a whiff, know what I mean?'"

Matron and Stephen burst out laughing. Stephen said, "Well, it's an old saying in the East End. If they won't bury you out of love, they'll have to bury you because of the stink."

Jeannette continued her story. "'Oh my God,' Aunt Masie, Uncle Frank's wife, said, 'We'll have yer mam in the front room for the rest of our lives and never get rid of her.'

"'No worry about that, ma'am. Smith and Bro. do not abandon a deceased halfway through the process. We'll pop her out the window.'

"So, they take the front window out, and they have to take the beading out as well, and they get the coffin through the window, Aunt Masie supervising, telling them not to scratch the paintwork. They load me Nan up on the hearse and get ready to drive off. Uncle Frank says, 'What about this window here? Ain't you putting it back?'

"'We're undertakers, mate,' the man says, 'not carpenters.'

"Off they go to the funeral, and Aunt Masie says she's not leaving her house open to thieves and the weather. She's houseproud, me Aunt Masie. Then Uncle Frank says, 'You're going to be worrying about all yer tat when they're putting me mam into the ground?'

"First they think they'll leave me to guard the house and the window. In my opinion, there was a lot more chance of somebody stealing the window than me Aunt Masie's collection of little china dogs. But I put up a cry. I want to see me Nan off so the neighbor next door says she'll have her eldest guard the place. He weren't going to the funeral anyway."

"I do like a good funeral," Matron said. "One where the person being buried had a good long life and you have a nice spread afterward and remember them. And a good story. They'll talk about your Nan's funeral for years, Jeannette."

"Who put the window back?" Stephen asked.

Jeannette said. "Uncle Frank did it as soon as he got back from the burial. He's knacky."

Matron left and sat at her desk, filling in forms. Stephen took out his shiny silver pencil and wrote to his brother. Jeannette lay in bed, remembering what happened after the funeral.

I could make a funny story about that, too, she thought. *It weren't funny, but I could make it funny. That funny little ugly skinny girl, all dressed in her best for the funeral, called down to the family meeting after the funeral. All the uncles and aunts sitting there with a bit of drink. I pranced in, like the Queen o' the May, excited about meeting me mother at last. Me mother, working in Southampton 'cause she didn't even want to be in the same city as me. Me mother, who looked as beautiful as any cinema star, me mother, that I thought would take me back to Southampton with her.*

I thought it was the shame of having a baby and no husband that made her leave me with me Nan. I thought I could tell her she could tell people I was her youngest sister and then we'd be together. I thought she'd probably been missing me.

So in I walked in, me new white dress bought special for the funeral, with me little straw hat, me white gloves, me new shoes, me hair done in corkscrew curls like Shirley Temple, and I sit down and nobody wanted to look at me.

Uncle Frank said they've been talking about me, where I'm going to live. I said I thought I'd live with me mother now. I could pretend to be her younger sister. I thought that was so clever, that little lie.

Aunt Masie said, 'See, that's the proper place for her. It's time you grew up and took some responsibility for your mistakes."

Me mother just laughed. 'The creature's nothing to me,' she said. 'You can put it on the streets or in an orphanage or drown it in the Thames. I came back for me mother's funeral, and now I'm off again, alone, the same way I came.'

Then me mother walked out and they started arguing about who would take me on. Uncle Frank lost, so I moved in with him.

Chapter Five

For a change, Sophie wasn't waving her hand madly in every class, volunteering the answer. She looked tired.

At lunch, Jean Marie asked her what was wrong.

"I didn't get much sleep last night," Sophie said. She shivered. "Last night, I could see this red glow outside the window. Irregular. I thought at first it was a car's brake lights reflected off one of the trailers. Then I realized it was a cigarette, somebody smoking, watching our trailer."

"Did you call the police?"

"I woke my mother up, suggested she call the police. Instead, she got the baseball bat she keeps for protection, threw open the door, and told whoever was there to come out. It was the new boyfriend, Cory."

"Creepy."

"Very creepy. He said he was there to protect us. A woman on her own, anything could happen. My mother shook the bat at him and said she could defend herself. He laughed. Then he pushed his way in and said he might as well protect her sitting on the sofa since she knew he was there."

"Your mother let him?"

"She ended up laughing and the two kept me awake."

"Bummer," Jean Marie said noncommittally.

"Sometimes, I like my mother's boyfriends. Sometimes, I don't like them. It doesn't make much difference either way. But this one, this Cory, I'm afraid of him. He wants to move in. I got my mother to promise she wouldn't let him. But she's not much for promises. She says conditions change."

After a minute, Sophie said, "I'm glad my mother said we couldn't afford food for a little kitten or a puppy. He's the kind of person that would kick it. Come on, let's walk around outside and get some fresh air before classes start."

That night, at dinner, Jean Marie said, "Do you ever think I ruined your life?"

Her mother laughed. "No, sometimes I think you may be trying, but I shall prevail. Of course not. You make my life much more pleasant. Whatever made you ask that?"

"Sometimes Sophie's mother tells her she ruined her life."

"Sophie's mother is twenty-six years old. She has plenty of time to change her life if she's not satisfied with it. That's not the only way her mother feels. Her mother boasts about Sophie, Sophie enjoys taking care of her mother. Sometimes Sophie and her mother get along very well."

"Well, sometimes I find your commonsense irritating. But, times like this, it's very comforting."

"Good."

"Sophie says this boyfriend is different. She's afraid of him."

"More common sense, the kind you find irritating: Sophie is stuck. She's got to get along with the man. Her mother's boyfriends don't last long. Remind her of that."

"Do you think she could stay with us? Just until her mother gets rid of the guy? We've got the room."

"Her mother would be insulted and angry if we invited Sophie to move in. There're things you can't do anything about, and I'm afraid this is one of them."

"I don't see why her mother has to have all these boyfriends. You get along perfectly fine without one."

"Not my choice, Jean Marie."

"You're not that old, or that bad looking…" She broke off as her mother started laughing.

"Thank you for the vote of confidence. It's a lack of time and opportunity. I work shifts at the library, with a lot of overtime. I work mainly with women. The men are either married or gay. However, there is somebody I've been having coffee with. He teaches English, we worked together on a library project celebrating Shakespeare's Anniversary. He asked me out to dinner Friday night."

"No babysitter. I can ask Sophie over to spend the night, we'll be fine on our own. You bring him in, we check him out. Sophie is a very good judge of character. What's his name?"

"Tim."

***

Stephen was helping Jeannette with her math when Mr. Finkelstein came in. She was glad he interrupted them. The hospital teacher said her reading was "adequate" but her math was very inadequate. Stephen had volunteered to help.

At least once in every session, he said, "But any idiot…" Mr. Finkelstein had heard that once and said, "Stephen, people are good at different things."

Stephen had said, "Except Jeannette."

He said he was only joking, but he wasn't. He meant it. She could add, subtract, multiply, and divide and usually get the right answer.

Today, Mr. Finkelstein brought her a present, a dictionary, to keep. She could look up the words she didn't know when she was reading.

"I can usually figure out what they mean, but this is better. Better to be sure."

Mr. Finkelstein left not long after Stephen went to physiotherapy. Jeannette opened her book and started reading. Stephen was exhausted when he got back, so she left him alone and continued reading.

It was almost dark when Jeannette shut her book, finished.

"This hospital really is a good place," she said to Stephen. "All the food I want, I like school lessons, now I can read, and your father brings me library books."

"All fiction," Stephen said. "Don't you have any interest in the real world?"

"No. It's nasty. If you could crawl into any book and live in it, which would you choose?"

"H. G. Wells, The Time Machine. I wouldn't go all the way to the end, but I'd like to see what is going to happen in the next couple of hundred years. It's going to be exciting."

"I'd choose a boring book, one with no excitement at all. The Bobbsey Twins, maybe."

Jeannette pulled her covers over her head. Sleep, eat, read. That and talking to Mr. Finkelstein and Stephen. This was the best it had ever been. She'd rather have a machine to stop time than go bouncing around.

Jeannette thought of Jean Marie then, the girl who had it so easy, the girl that thought she was some kind of nasty creature, an 'it', and dismissed her as a liar and a thief.

Suddenly, she was in Jean Marie's head, looking through Jean Marie's eyes. She wasn't asleep and dreaming. She was awake. So was Jean Marie.

"You think I'm a thief and a liar, do you? You stupid cow. You think you're so much better than me. You're not. You're just lucky."

For a moment, Jeannette felt like the world stood still. Then everything changed.

She knew Jean Marie heard her.

Then she felt satisfaction. *So, let her know what I think of her.* Jeannette laughed to herself.

Then she heard the commotion in the hall.

"Dr. Baron! Dr. Baron can't be dead."

The orderly said, "Somebody smashed her over the head, stole the money she was taking to the poor, and the drugs. Everybody knew her, even the hard men in the area liked her. Must be some druggie…"

No, my Uncle Richard, he'd do that. Me Nan always said he wasn't as bad as people thought, but she was his mother. She had to think that. That's what all mothers, except mine, think.

Chapter Six

Hearing voices? Voices in my head? Voices I can barely understand because they've got an English accent? Jean Marie said aloud, "Not voices, one voice. Jeannette." Jean Marie did not want to think of the pain in the voice. So, she's miserable, so what? she thought. It's not my fault.

How had Jeannette spoken to her? She dreamed about Jeannette, Jeannette dreamed about her. They didn't talk to each other. If she can get into my head, I should be able to get into hers. Jean Marie focused on Jeannette. Nothing happened. After a few minutes, she thought, How can she speak to me when I can't speak to her?

She couldn't speak to Jeannette, but Jean Marie realized she was in touch with her. There were scenes. A woman was slapping her and shouting: "I knew you'd bring bad luck into this house. You're sick, you've brought sickness into this house with your nasty ways."

I don't care, Jean Marie thought. I hate her, and the woman's right. Nasty little creature. I don't want to understand her. I want her out of my head.

There's more than one way to communicate. Jean Marie picked up a felt tip pin and wrote on a large sheet of paper: "Stay out of my head. You're stupid, ugly, a thief, and a liar. Nobody wants you around, especially me."

She taped the note over her bed.

Jean Marie picked up the phone and called Sophie. A man answered the telephone and said, "Hello."

Jean Marie hesitated. She had speed-dialed; she couldn't have the wrong number. She said, "This is Jean Marie. May I speak to Sophie, please?"

"What do you want Sophie for?"

"To talk to," she said. What business is it of his?

"She's busy. You can talk to her tomorrow." The man hung up the phone.

Jean Marie started to re-dial the number, then hung up the telephone.

She wandered into the living room and sat down. Her mother was reading.

"Mom," she said, "I called Sophie and her mother's boyfriend answered the phone. He wouldn't let me talk to Sophie. He said I could talk to her at school, tomorrow. He said she was busy."

"Maybe she was. You just spent the weekend together. She only left here a few hours ago."

"I've got a bad feeling about him."

"Don't encourage Sophie with your 'bad feelings'. If he's part of her mother's life, she's going to have to get along with him."

"That's not fair."

"Nope," her mother agreed.

The next morning, Jean Marie saw Sophie in the hall and pushed through the crowd of students to join her.

Jean Marie said, "Guess what happened…" She stopped talking. "Sophie, you look awful."

"I look the same way I always do."

"No, you don't."

Sophie had always reminded Jean Marie of a terrier, a scruffy little terrier with bright eyes, alert, curious, interested in anything the world had to offer.

"I'm tired, that's all. I was up most of the night."

"Were you sick?"

"No. We've got to get to class. I'll tell you about it at lunch."

At lunch, Sophie told Jean Marie what happened. "The boyfriend's moved in. All his junk is piled in my room."

"Bummer," Jean Marie said cautiously.

"We picked up some fried chicken on the way home. After we ate, he and my mom drank some beer and watched TV. I washed the dishes and started doing my homework. My mom went to bed. About ten, he came into my room and said the kitchen wasn't clean enough. I had to do it right."

She showed Jean Marie her swollen, red hands. "He made me use bleach, right out of the bottle, and a scrub brush to clean the counters, the cupboards, the floor, the whole kitchen. Straight bleach is not good for your hands."

"Your hands look sore."

"They are. They burn and itch."

"Why don't you go to the school nurse and get something for them?"

"And tell her what? I don't want anybody to know about this, especially not your mom. It's humiliating."

"Tell the nurse you decided to scrub the kitchen and were stupid enough to use pure bleach. There's nothing humiliating about that."

"Maybe."

"No 'maybe'. Your hands could get infected. Don't be stupid. And what happened to your glasses?"

"He came in to inspect the floor. He said my glasses weren't any good since I couldn't see all the filth and he broke them." Sophie started to cry. "I can't see. These are bifocals, and I have to shift my eyes for close stuff and far stuff. They're out of alignment, and my mom says she can't afford new ones."

"The lenses are what cost the most. You can get new frames pretty cheap."

"I started yelling when he took my glasses. My mother woke up. It was about three o'clock in the morning. She said she had to be at work at 6 a.m. and stop all the noise."

"That's all your mom said?"

"Well, she told me to stop squealing and him to stop being a horse's ass. Then she went back to bed. I went to bed, and when I got up this morning, he was asleep on the sofa, TV still going."

"Come on. I'll go with you to the nurse's office."

The nurse put some ointment on Sophie's hands and gave her a pair of clear plastic gloves to wear.

"No writing for a couple of days," the nurse said. "I'll send round a note to your teachers. You're homework free for a day or two, Sophie. Always wear rubber gloves when you're using cleaning products. You might be allergic to bleach. Didn't you notice it burning your hands?"

"It hurt a little, but I didn't think it would do this."

"If something hurts, stop. You should see a doctor about this. Who's your family doctor?"

"We don't have one," Sophie said.

The nurse said, "You really should see a doctor. See the blisters on your hands? They're going to break, and if they get infected it can be very serious. If the area around feels hot, or you see purple or black streaks, go to the emergency room immediately. I'm going to give you some antibiotic cream and some more plastic gloves. Wash the hands in cool water, dry them carefully with a clean towel, and put on the cream. Come in tomorrow and let me look at your hands."

After they left the nurse's office, Jean Marie said abruptly, "Something else. New development on the Jeannette front."

"What?"

"Voices. In my head while I'm awake. She spoke to me, yelled at me, actually, and said I was a selfish brat, lucky, no better than her."

"Interesting," Sophia said.

"Voices in my head, Sophie. Dreams, I can handle. But voices? Everybody dreams, but schizos and loonies hear voices in their heads."

"You're not crazy," Sophie said.

"Are you sure?"

"Of course, I'm sure."

***

"But I don't understand why you're so upset," Stephen said.

"You don't understand," Jeannette said.

"That's what I just said, I don't understand. Your imaginary friend hates you. So what? Create a better one. For heaven's sake! With all that's going on, you're crying about some stupid dream."

The hospital was crowded. Last night, the German planes had come in wave after wave, in a continuous bombardment of the East End of London. All the available beds were full, and patients were sleeping on stretchers in the halls. Matron checked on them in the morning, and an orderly had brought them some bread, cheese, and an apple for the noon meal. Jeannette had been crying most of the day.

"Jean Marie hates me. She thinks she understands why we're dreaming of each other's lives, and I think she's right."

Stephen waited for Jeannette to continue. The room was dark, and he couldn't see her. He heard the tired voice from the bed next to him.

"Jean Marie thinks she is me, I am her, at different times. She thinks that this, you and me in the hospital, are part of a past life that she has lived. She hates the idea. She doesn't want anything to do with me, because she thinks I'm a nothing. She hates the idea that she could be me."

Stephen said, "She's wrong about your dreams showing reincarnation. Maybe she'd dream about you, but that doesn't explain how you can dream about her. In reincarnation, after a person dies their soul is born in another body. You and the girl would have the same soul and you couldn't be alive at the same time."

"We're not alive at the same time. She's alive in the future. She sees things in my future. I can look at her looking at me and I see things that happen in the next couple of days or weeks. Why does she hate me so much? What's she seeing? What if I become a murderer? Or do something else really terrible?"

"Stop being such a drama queen," Stephen said impatiently. "You want to know what I really think? I think you had a telepathic experience with the speech. You caught Churchill writing it before he gave it. Nothing to do with the future. The rest, well, I think all these people are something you imagined. They're parts of yourself, and Jean Marie dislikes you because you dislike parts of yourself."

The wail of the aircraft siren interrupted Stephen. Jeannette tried to imagine what it was like outside, on the streets of London. It had been almost a year since she had come into the hospital. Her aunt and uncle had disappeared. No one knew where they were.

Stephen's father said people went down into the underground when the sirens blew. He was a volunteer fire warden and helped put out fires after the bombs. He made jokes about his little tin hat. He said he hated the looters worse than the bombs.

"Scum," he said. "Scum that steal from their own during the blackout. It's as if London has an underworld of vermin that take over the city during the bombings."

Jeannette felt uncomfortable. She suspected some of her uncles might be part of the increased crime rate. Not her Uncle Frank. Frank worked down on the docks, and if a crate broke, well, that was part of the perks of being a docker. Her Uncle Richard, on the other hand, was a bit of a hard man who worked for a harder man. When she was little, she'd asked him once what he did.

"A bit o' this, a bit o' that, love," he'd said.

When he walked down the street, people shifted out of his way. She'd asked her Nan about it, and her Nan had been vague.

"People talk, don't they, love? Gossip, something I don't hold with. They always exaggerate. Your Uncle Richard has a heart of gold, pure gold. He loves his family, he does. Richard and Frank might not get on, but Richard would be the first one there if your Uncle Frank needed anything."

Uncle Richard had come to her Nan's laying out after she'd gone to bed. He'd come to the funeral and the graveyard. He hadn't come back to the house afterward. They'd talked about it, and Uncle Frank had spit on the ground. "Good riddance to bad rubbish."

She'd repeated what her Nan had said and Uncle Frank laughed. "He'd help all right," her uncle said, "and he'd have his pound of flesh after. It'll be a cold day in hell before I ask anything from that one."

Yes, her Uncle Richard would be out there, in the dark, slithering and slying between the bombs dropping, doing a little o' this, a little o' that.

There was taking something that wasn't exactly stealing, more boosting your pay packet, what you should have been given anyway. Uncle Frank came home with a box of dates once, from a broken crate. *Like cockroaches without legs,* she'd thought when she saw them. But they were tasty. Very tasty. That wasn't stealing. That was taking advantage. Then there was real stealing, breaking into a shop or a house. Uncle Richard was the only one of her family that really stole things.

That's something Jean Marie can't understand, Jeannette thought. She was fairly sure that Mr. Finkelstein and Stephen would have a hard time understanding it as well.

"Thought I'd keep the pair of you company." Franz wheeled himself into the room. He was a Czech pilot and had come to Britain and joined the RAF after the fall of Czechoslovakia. His plane had been shot down over Surrey in June and he'd come to the hospital for an operation on his broken leg.

The sirens stopped and the noise of the incoming bombers took over.

"War is so loud," Jeannette said. You could hear the sound of the airplanes first, then the sound of the bombs exploding.

Jeannette saw Paul, the physiotherapist, and one of the orderlies open the fire exit door. During attacks, two people sat on the roof and put out any incendiary bombs that landed. Paul had volunteered.

The sound of planes grew fainter. It was, at least, a lull. They still might come back tonight.

"Our planes are better," Stephen said.

Franz shrugged. "Better, yes, I think so. Their medium bombers, the Stuka and the Heinkel, are fast. Very good for supporting their ground troops, but not so good for this campaign. They're vulnerable to the RAF attack. The spitfire is better than the Messerschmidt."

Franz rolled a cigarette and lit it. "They don't have the fuel reserves. A Messerschmidt can spend about 15 minutes after it arrives in London, then must turn back. The Stuka is exposed. They have more planes than we do, but we shoot down more. They lose many more pilots than we do. They're fighting over unfriendly territory. My friend, his plane was shot down over Kent. Lucky. He didn't break a leg. He landed with his parachute and the people in the village took him to the pub, all insisted on buying him a pint, then gave him a ride back to base. German pilots, they ditch in the channel and are drowned."

"I wish we could bomb Berlin like they're bombing London," Jeannette said.

"Foolishness," Franz answered. "At first, in June and July, the Germans bombed the convoys in the Channel, the airfields in Kent and Surrey. That was truly damaging us. Then they change to bomb London. They think it will break morale. It won't, but it gives us a breathing space to build more planes, train more pilots. I suspect it is Hitler himself that grew impatient and ordered the cities to be bombed. Politicians are politicians, not generals. They should keep their noses out of the war."

In the distance, they heard the drone of the second wave of bombers growing closer. "Listen carefully," Franz said. "You can hear something low and dark, Stuka. Something higher, like a mosquito, Messerschmidt. Something higher still, and fast and gay and beautiful. Like a Mozart symphony. My plane. The spitfire."

Stephen laughed. "I've heard Mozart, and it doesn't sound anything like a spitfire."

"Metaphorically, my boy, metaphorically." Franz winked at Stephen. "At least, the sound of a well-flying spitfire causes the same joy in my heart as the opening of a Mozart concerto."

Jeannette pulled the covers over her head. *If a bomb's got my name on it,* she thought, *I'm dead and there's nothing I can do about it. I might as well try to sleep. I'd rather die asleep than awake.* As the drone of airplanes and the sound of bombs exploding mixed with the laughter of Franz and Stephen, Jeannette thought, *Men are crazy.*

Jeannette was dreaming. She realized, surprised, that Jean Marie was dreaming as well. She observed The Dream. She saw the hospital room, her hospital room, and it was daytime. She and Stephen were eating breakfast.

59

Matron, Paul, and a policeman came to the door of their room. Matron said, "Jeannette, Paul has time to give you an extra session this morning." Jeannette knew something had happened to Mr. Finkelstein.

Chapter Seven

Jeannette left the room. Jean Marie continued to look at the scene. Matron and a policeman stood in the doorway.

I'm seeing this myself, it's not Jeannette's memories, and I'm not seeing it through Jeannette's eyes.

Jean Marie did not want to watch the scene.

Stephen sat up in bed. He looked grim, stern. *This is how he'll look when he's a man,* Jean Marie thought. *I don't want to hear this, I want to go home, back to my time and my place. Stephen doesn't want to hear this, either.*

"Something's happened, Matron," Stephen said.

Matron and the policeman walked into the room and stood at the foot of Stephen's bed.

Stephen said. "My father, is he hurt? Or is it worse?"

"A second wave of bombers came while the firemen were still dealing with the first," the policeman said.

The policeman's voice wavered from exhaustion. Jean Marie realized the man could barely stand up.

"Please sit down, sir," Stephen said.

The policeman took off his helmet and sat down on the chair at the end of Stephen's bed. "The whole East End is up in flames," he said. "Lad, it's all burning. Your father was out there in it with the firemen. I knew him, your father. I wanted to come myself to tell you, answer any questions. Somebody had been storing petrol. A lot of it. A black marketeer, probably. Your father was holding the hose. The petrol exploded. The blast took the wall out, and your father was in the way of it. He didn't know a thing. It was very, very quick."

"He didn't burn?" Stephen whispered.

61

"On my word. It was quick and he never knew what hit him."

"Thank you," Stephen said. "Thank you for coming and telling me."

Jean Marie opened her eyes and looked around at her familiar room. She slept through the alarm clock. Today was her mother's day to open the library at seven, and her mother would be gone.

So that's war. Stephen was brave. But what else could he be? If it were my father or my mother, I think I'd scream. I don't think I could be so polite.

Jean Marie got up. She had twenty minutes before the school bus came. She let the dog into the back yard and fed the cat. *I'd like to go back to bed, sleep and sleep and sleep, with no dreams and no one watching,* Jean Marie thought. If she hadn't been worried about Sophie, she would have said she was sick and sat all day in front of the television eating potato chips and drinking Coke.

Instead, she called the dog inside, gathered up her books, and went to the bus stop.

She met Sophie walking to history.

Jean Marie said. "How are your hands?"

"They hurt, but not as much as they did. I saw the nurse this morning, and she said they looked good. She called my mother at work yesterday to tell her I needed to see a doctor."

"What did your mother say?"

"She told the nurse she didn't have a hundred dollars to take me to the emergency ward."

"No doctor?"

"No money."

"What about the boyfriend?"

"Still there."

"I know. I called last night."

Sophie looked at Jean Marie and smiled. "I didn't know you called. I kept expecting you to call, and when you didn't, well, I'm glad to know you did."

"Of course I called. I wanted to know what the doctor said. The boyfriend answered and said you couldn't talk on the phone."

At lunchtime, Jean Marie joined Sophie. Sophie was more cheerful.

"I saw the nurse this morning, and she changed the dressing. She said the hands were doing nicely."

"Where's your lunch?"

"We were out of bread so I couldn't make a sandwich."

Jean Marie separated her chicken nuggets and french fries into two piles.

"Eat," she told Sophie.

"That's your lunch."

"Don't be stupid. Eat. I've got a lot to tell you or I'd make you take some money and buy lunch."

Sophie laughed. "You can be such a bully, J.M."

"For your own good."

They ate Jean Marie's lunch and went outside where they could talk privately. Sophie listened to all that had happened.

"Do you think the policeman was telling the truth about it being quick, painless?" Jean Marie asked.

"Who knows? He should have said it even if it were a lie," Sophie said. "You're really upset about the father dying, aren't you?"

"I know them, Sophie. These are people I know as well as I know you."

"It was a long time ago," Sophie said.

"It was last night. I was there. I saw them and heard them."

"Jeannette wasn't there?"

"No, I told you, she left the room."

"Then you watched Stephen after Jeannette left the room. You could see it independently."

"Right." Jean Marie hesitated. "Jeannette and I are the same. Me and Jeannette, I thought it was reincarnation, that maybe I was remembering her life. But she can talk to me. I can see things she didn't see. Now, I don't know. I don't understand this at all.

"It's not just me and Jeannette. Some of the people there, I know them and I know them in this life, not that one. I don't always know who they are, but I'm sure I know them. Sometimes, I do know. The school nurse and the Matron in their hospital are the same people."

"Mr. Finkelstein, Stephen's father. Do you think you know him? Maybe that's why you're taking this so personally."

"Sometimes Mr. Finkelstein reminds me of my mother," Jean Marie said. "I keep thinking of how I'd feel if my mother died. It's like there are two present times running side by side, the same people with different bodies. It's all present for me, not sixty-five years ago."

"Nobody knows how time works anyway," Sophie said.

"Of course we do. It's one damned thing after another."

Sophie laughed and said, "A good working definition for practical purposes, but I don't think philosophers or physicists would find it very helpful."

"If it's reincarnation, it's religion, not science."

"Imagine," Sophie said, "imagine energy changing into matter. Physics. Now imagine souls becoming bodies. Religion. Both are talking about a relationship between two kinds of things. Souls and bodies, energy, and mass."

Sophie gazed into the distance, lost in thought, her mouth open.

"Soph, Soph," Jean Marie said.

"I'm sorry," Sophie said. "It was like I could see a pattern, not words, but a visual pattern. It was like a huge fishing net thrown across the universe made of points of space-time. Mass has three dimensions: depth, width, and height. Add time to that as the fourth dimension. Time isn't something independent, outside space. Time is how we describe a change in a system.

"The smallest particles of matter scientists have found are quarks and leptons. Those plus the way they interact are the building blocks of the universe. Little squiggly quarks decaying, forming, because a couple have come together and are interacting. That's time for you, J.M., the change in a quark.

"At the other end, we've got gravity and electromagnetism, the great huge things, the forces that bend the universe, make it curve on itself.

"We're somewhere in the middle. The universe is a system, too. If we could step back, somehow be external to the system, we could see more space-time points. The time that we experience is only local. At the level of atoms and molecules, the gold necklace you find in a Pharaoh's tomb is the same necklace made of the same gold. At the level of the quark, it's not. All kinds of change have been going on. The advertisement says diamonds are forever. They're not forever, but they remain diamonds considerably longer than we remain people.

"When we look at people, we know cells live and die and change and you've gotten different cells than you had when you were born. You're still Jean Marie; quarks, cells, tissues, organs, and a body. This Jean Marie is conscious of being Jean Marie, and that's why we say we're the same, even though the cells that make us aren't the same. It's consciousness that is the same, not the body.

"Some bundles of cells are conscious. Maybe everything, maybe rocks and gravity and all the rest of it have some kind of awareness. Maybe that is preserved, independent of the body. It changes, but there is something that remains. You and Jeannette aren't really the same person, you know. But there is something that is the same. That part ties you together and you communicate."

Sophie continued. "The fifth dimension. Consciousness. Rocks and water and dogs and people, just consciousness."

"That's…" Jean Marie hesitated, "Interesting. But it's not very useful, Sophie."

"You're right," Sophie said cheerfully. "The fifth dimension business is about as interesting as believing the world sits on the back of a giant turtle. But it's potentially more interesting because it's got more scope than the turtle."

"I dunno," Jean Marie said. "The giant turtle could be sitting on the back of a more giant elephant."

"Ah," said Sophie. "But what's the elephant sitting on?"

"He's Dumbo, flapping his ears and flying. That's what causes the planets to move. The wind caused by Dumbo's ears."

"Sounds good to me," Sophie said. "But I think you better plan on establishing a new religion instead of a new science. The flapping ear model of the universe might explain helicopters, but the standard model of force and reaction works better with jet engines."

"Enough fooling around," Jean Marie said. "I'll stick to reincarnation until you think of something better."

The bell rang and the girls stood up to walk to class.

"At least you don't explain all this by telling me I'm crazy," Jean Marie said.

Jean Marie met Sophie after their last class, and they walked towards the school buses waiting in the parking lot. Sophie's bus driver insisted on promptness. People sat in their seats. No yelling. No shoving. He closed the doors of the bus fifteen minutes after classes ended and pulled out three minutes later. When he shut the door, he didn't open it. Once he'd left a child banging on the bus doors to get in. He'd just started the bus and driven away. Jean Marie's mother had laughed when she heard the story and said she didn't believe it. But everyone knew it was true.

"Oh, no," Sophie said. "The boyfriend."

Jean Marie saw an old car, a banged-up convertible, with a man standing beside it smoking a cigarette.

"Quick," Sophie said, "I'll pretend I didn't see him and get on the bus."

But the man saw them and pushed his way through the crowd of children.

"Wait up," he called. "Wait up, Sophie."

Sophie stood next to her bus. She looked smaller. Jean Marie thought she looked afraid.

The boyfriend was short, not much taller than Jean Marie. He was muscular, and Jean Marie thought he probably worked out in the gym. His pale grey eyes and blonde, almost white, eyelashes and hair contrasted with his tan. *He should be good looking,* Jean Marie thought. *Great body, nothing wrong with his face. Nothing I can identify and say why he reminds me of a snake. Or something worse than a snake. I like snakes. Maybe a really well-fed sleek rat, a self-satisfied wharf rat, not a little field mouse that moved into the kitchen. Anyone with any sense would look at him and run. Nothing wrong with him at all, except he terrifies me. No wonder Sophie's afraid.*

The boyfriend smiled at Jean Marie.

"This must be the famous Jean Marie that I talk to every night. Ain't it odd how pretty girls always have ugly best friends?" he said.

He said that to make Sophie feel bad, Jean Marie thought. She tried to think of something clever, something that would put him in his place. She stood silently.

Sophie looked at the ground. A crowd of children had gathered outside the door to the bus. They stood watching.

"I was in the neighborhood so I came to give you a ride home, Sophie," he said.

The bus driver got off the bus and stood next to Sophie. He was a large man with a tattoo on his upper arm. Jean Marie was glad he was a lot bigger than the boyfriend.

"Get on the bus, Sophie," he said.

"She doesn't need to ride the bus today, friend. I come to give her a ride home."

"She's riding the school bus home," the bus driver said. "School regulations."

Mrs. Adams, the math teacher, came up then. She said, "Is there a problem?"

The boyfriend smiled. "No problem, ma'am. I'm Cody Johnston, Sophie's mama's fiancé, and I've come to give her a ride home. So we could have a little quality time, get to know each other better."

The smile was not reassuring. Jean Marie drew a little closer to the bus driver.

"I'm sorry, Mr. Johnston, but the school cannot allow any student to leave with anyone but their legal guardian. I'm sure you understand," Mrs. Adams said. She put her hand on Sophie's shoulder. "Sophie, get on the school bus."

"That goes for the rest of you," the bus driver said. "On the bus."

The children filed on the bus. Jean Marie saw Sophie take a window seat, watching.

Cody smiled again. He said, softly, to the bus driver, "I won't forget this, friend."

The bus driver leaned towards him and said just as quietly, "I'm not your friend. And I'm not a little girl that's scared of you. Remember anything you want, you little pissant."

Jean Marie, the bus driver, and Mrs. Adams watched the man walk back to his car and start it.

"He's horrible," Jean Marie said.

The bus driver laughed. "Nah. He's a little pissant, and you know what you do with pissants, don't you? You step on 'em."

"Haven't you got a bus to catch, Jean Marie?" Mrs. Adams said.

As Jean Marie walked back to her bus, she thought, *Uncle Richard's shown up.*

***

Stephen was furious. "I do not want to listen to this," he said. "No more. Nothing is going to happen to my father. I don't know whether you believe what you say or not, and I don't care."

Jeannette felt helpless. "I don't know what the people that came into the room told you. It was Matron, Paul, and a policeman. If it had been something wrong with your brother, your father would have come. I thought your father was hurt."

"You said 'dead' before."

"I said maybe, I didn't know."

"Premonitions now. You're just trying to make yourself important."

Stephen and Jeannette heard footsteps in the hall. The footsteps were slow and steady.

"One set of footsteps, not three," Stephen said. "Not Matron's."

Stephen's father stood in the doorway. He looked very tired.

Jeannette said, "You're all right, you're all right."

Mr. Finkelstein sat down in the chair beside Jeannette's bed. He took out his handkerchief and poured a little water on it from the pitcher next to the bed.

"You've been crying," he said, "and your eyes are all swollen." He wiped her eyes and face with the wet handkerchief and said, "Blow."

Jeannette blew her nose.

"She's got the attention she wants, so she's happy now," Stephen said.

"Perhaps she needs attention," Mr. Finkelstein said. "What's the matter now, love? Are you in pain?"

"I thought you were dead."

"No, no. I'm fine. I'm tired, it was a hard night, but I'm all right."

"We didn't see you for two days, two whole days," Stephen said.

"The bombs have been coming in waves, during the day as well as the night. I've been on duty. One plane after the other. I haven't been home, I haven't been to work. I've been on my route, walking the streets, looking for fires, for survivors, for looters. Jeannette, Stephen, I'm sorry you were worried."

"I wasn't worried. I knew you were all right," Stephen said. "I knew it was something like that. Madam Blavatsky here, she has premonitions. She has dreams. She can take her damned dreams and…"

"Stephen!" His father interrupted him. "We all have bad dreams. We're all afraid they're true. Jeannette is a dear, sensitive child. You're almost a man, and you should reassure her, not attack her."

A dear, sensitive child. Jeannette thought. *He called me a dear child.* Mr. Finkelstein put his arm around her and she leaned against his shoulder. She felt Mr. Finkelstein's wool jacket scratching her cheek. For a moment, Jeannette felt safe.

"I haven't done anything," Stephen said. "I haven't tried to terrify people by claiming their father was dead. She goes on and on about her stupid dreams where she sees the future."

"You have to admit I was right about the one thing we could check," Jeannette said. "Even you admit I couldn't have known it."

Jeannette and Stephen, interrupting each other, told Mr. Finkelstein about the Prime Minister's speech, about Sophie and Jean Marie.

Mr. Finkelstein frowned, he thought, then he said, "Jeannette, you read Prime Minister Churchill's speech in this girl's history book?"

"Yes," Jeannette said. "I remembered it because it was beautiful."

"It's a speech that will go into history books if we win the war," Mr. Finkelstein said.

"Oh, we'll win," Jeannette said. "We'll win completely. Germany will invade Russia, the United States will come into the war, we'll win all right. That's in the history books, too."

"How do you explain the speech, Stephen?"

"Telepathy. That part we can verify, that's objective."

"So, you'll pick through what Jeannette says and take what you want and reject the rest? That doesn't sound very objective."

"So, Poppa, tell me how she can see the future?"

"I don't know," Mr. Finkelstein said. "But there are large numbers of things I don't know. Mr. Einstein, Mr. Einstein writes about time being relative."

"Oh, Poppa, you're so ignorant. You don't understand Mr. Einstein's Theory. You don't have the background in physics or mathematics to have the slightest notion of what he's talking about. An hour's lecture at the Workman's Institute and reading Professor Russell's book aren't enough to make you an authority."

Jeannette had been watching Mr. Finkelstein's face. It was, she thought, a beautiful face. *You can always tell what he's thinking,* she thought. When Stephen called his father ignorant, Mr. Finkelstein's face became immobile, like a mask. *Stephen hurt his father dreadfully,* Jeannette thought, *dreadfully. How could he do that?*

"Stephen," Jeannette said, "you are a very rude boy."

"I am sure you are right, and I do not understand Mr. Einstein's Theory of General Relativity," Mr. Finkelstein said. "I am also sure that you cannot pick and choose the information you think is important and dismiss the rest of it as nonsense. If you wish, you can say that you cannot explain the rest of Jeannette's dreams. But you have no evidence that she is lying."

"She's lied about other things. Once a liar, always a liar. But I don't claim she's lying," Stephen said. "I think she's crazy."

Paul stuck his head in the door. "Stephen," he said, "it's been three days since you've had physiotherapy. During this lull, why don't we put a session in? Mr. Finkelstein, why don't you kip out on the cot in the Staff Room? Matron suggested it. You can get some sleep before the next round of bombs hit us."

Paul brought the wheelchair into the room and shifted Stephen into it. "Another couple of sessions and you'll have crutches and make your own way," he said.

"Fine," Stephen said. "We'll leave these two to tell each other fairy tales."

Stephen and Paul left the room.

Mr. Finkelstein said. "Stephen reacts with anger when he's afraid. He was afraid you were right, and so he attacked you."

"I know," Jeannette said. "That didn't bother me. But he shouldn't have said those things to you."

Mr. Finkelstein said, "But he was right. I am an ignorant old man. That's the problem with being an autodidact." He looked down and kissed the top of Jeannette's head. "An autodidact is someone who teaches himself. I'm like a magpie, picking up this shiny new idea and that one, with blank spots, trying to understand what I read. Stephen will understand and know more than I ever will. That's what parents want, you know. They want their children to be better in every way than they are."

"Stephen may know more, but he'll never be as wise as you are," Jeannette said.

"You're very kind, and I'm flattered. I hope you'll both be wiser as well as know more than I do. He also has a bad habit of thinking that what he knows is the only important thing to know. Stephen can be a bit intolerant, my dear. Don't let him bully you."

"I don't," Jeannette said. "He doesn't try, much. Stephen knows more than I do about some things, but not everything."

"You are very capable of learning the same things Stephen does. Your tutor is impressed by how much you've learned."

Jeannette was delighted. "He is? He never tells me that."

"Tutors don't. He doesn't want you to become vain."

"I'd like a bit of being vain. I don't have a lot of chances."

Mr. Finkelstein laughed. "Of course you would. Personally, I think carrots are better than sticks. You need to be told you do well as well as badly. But your tutor is proud of your progress. He says you are ahead of your grade level and should do well when you go back into the classroom."

When I get out, there's no classroom to go to. There's the street. Jeannette felt the old fear coming back. She avoided thinking of leaving the hospital.

Mr. Finkelstein hesitated, then said, "Don't worry about the future, Jeannette. We haven't said anything about this to you, because we haven't been sure it can be arranged. But Matron and I have been very worried about where you'll go. Matron's from a small village in Wales, with a cottage hospital where her sister works. You'll stay in the hospital, and go to the village school at first, then you can live with her sister. I'll write you. I'm not going to forget about you, you know."

"When I'm fourteen, school ends." Jeannette said. "What then? I'm a cripple. What kind of work can I do?"

"You're an intelligent, talented young lady. You will probably always have a crutch and a brace. You can work in an office or a bank or do a number of other jobs. Your tutor thinks you should stay on in school until sixteen and go on for further study, at college. He thinks you would do very well with business studies or perhaps education, teaching in an infant school. There's a further education college in Greenwich. You can stay with me, in Stephen's room."

"That will cost a lot."

"Not much. Books, uniforms, bus fare. This is 1940. This war will be over, and we will win it. It's going to be a brave new world, and you are going to do well in it. The world is your oyster, young woman, and I forbid you to worry about the future. Matron and I have it well in hand."

"Yes, sir."

"Now, enough serious discussion. I'm going to find the cot Paul mentioned and you are going to sleep and you'll have pleasant dreams."

After Mr. Finkelstein left, Jeannette sank back in her bed, exhausted. The only future she had been able to imagine was sitting on the curb at Covent Garden, begging for pennies, having the police tell her to move on. *Matron and I have it well in hand, he said. Darling dear Mr. Finkelstein. Knowing that you wanted to take care of me is almost good enough. I am going to miss you dreadfully, Mr. Finkelstein. I wish you were my father. I don't believe in happy endings but knowing someone wanted a happy ending for me is strange, and good, and wonderful. I don't believe in brave new worlds. For Stephen maybe, he's special. But not for me.*

She heard Jean Marie's voice then.

Oh come off it, the voice said. *None of this pessimism. Unhappy endings are old fashioned. I saw Mr. Finkelstein's death reported, not you. Maybe I was wrong. Maybe the policeman was wrong. Maybe we changed the future and it won't happen. He's not dead yet. Remember, it ain't over till the fat lady sings.*

The voice faded away. *Maybe, but I don't think so,* Jeannette thought. She yawned. *If you think the worst is going to happen, you're never disappointed. My Nan taught me that.* Jeannette fell asleep and began to dream. She saw Jean Marie's room and Jean Marie had put another poster up. "I'm sorry," Jeannette read. "I don't hate you."

Jean Marie herself was sitting on the bed, eating a bowl of chocolate ice cream. Jean Marie looked up and winked.

Chapter Eight

When Jean Marie arrived at school, she saw people gathered in small groups. Some of the girls were crying. Dawn came up to her.

"Have you heard?"

"Heard what?" Jean Marie asked.

"Mr. Jenks, you know, the bus driver on the Southwest bus, the one your friend Sophie rides. He's in the hospital."

"That's terrible," Jean Marie said. *At his age,* Jean Marie thought*, a heart attack is most likely. That or an accident. He must be over fifty.* "What's wrong with him?"

"Nobody knows," Dawn said. "Just that he's in the hospital. The pep squad is going to take up a collection to send flowers."

Jean Marie saw two policemen coming out of the principal's office. A policewoman followed them. *Three cops, one a woman,* Jean Marie thought.

"They're here about Mr. Jenks," Sophie said.

Jean Marie turned around. "I didn't see you in the hall," she said. "Where did you come from?"

"School auditorium. We got herded in there when we got off the bus. The principal made an announcement. He said Mr. Jenks was attacked last night, and the police want to talk to everybody that rides his bus. They'll call some of us out of class, one by one."

"They think one of the kids did it?"

"They always think one of the kids did it. Usually a kid from our trailer park," Sophie said. "I think they're wrong. Everybody likes him. He coaches a Little League team, and they always do really well.

Everybody goes to the games they play by the trailer park. Even the high school kids show up. A kid didn't do this. I don't believe a kid could have. Mr. Jenks was a retired air force sergeant. He was big, tough, and kept in shape."

"Who do you think did it?"

"Maybe one of the drug dealers that want to use the park to sell stuff. Mr. Jenks has a little house that's across the street from the park. He pays attention and calls the police if any dealer tries to set up a base in the park."

As the morning went on, Jean Marie watched children leaving her class one by one. Most of the teachers ignored their usual lesson plans. They told the class to open their books and read or work in their workbooks. The math teacher had three sheets of problems she passed out. In history, the students were allowed to work in groups on a worksheet. Jean Marie joined Sophie. There was a buzz of quiet conversation in the room, and none of it was about history.

Softly, Jean Marie asked Sophie if she had trouble when she got home yesterday.

"You mean with Cory? I'd forgotten about that, and yes there was trouble. Cory didn't say anything about my not riding home with him, but my computer and printer were gone. He said some druggie from the trailer park must have broken in and stolen them."

"That's terrible."

Sophie said, "He didn't expect me to believe him. No druggie would take the computer and printer. He couldn't get more than five dollars for them if he could sell them at all. There was stuff in the trailer somebody actually could sell, but nothing else was taken. Not the TV, or my mom's guitar. My mom's hocked the guitar a couple of times. She got 150 dollars for it, and it's easy to carry. Any druggie would have taken that, not my computer and printer. Besides, nobody saw anybody around our trailer. Half the people in the trailer park are retired and don't have anything better to do than watch their neighbors.

Somebody would have noticed a kid breaking in during the day. Cory took them for payback. To show me what happens when I don't do exactly what he says."

"What did your mom say?"

"Complicated. She didn't say anything to Cory directly, but she told me later to be careful. 'Don't make Cory mad,' she said. He has a bad temper, which I already knew. She said he was on-edge because three people in a trailer is very crowded. I told her I'd noticed. Then she gave me ten dollars to buy my lunch for the rest of the week."

"She felt guilty about the computer."

"Maybe."

The PA system came on and they heard the principal's voice.

"Good morning, students. This is Mr. MacCrae. You all know the police have been interviewing some students this morning. Mr. Jenks, who drove the Southwest school bus, is in the hospital."

They heard Mr. MacCrae clear his throat and the PA buzzed. Unusually, no one laughed.

"Mr. Jenks woke up about 2 a.m. when he heard someone outside breaking his car windows. He got up and went out to challenge the intruder while his wife called the police. When the police arrived, they discovered Mr. Jenks had been attacked by the vandals and left by the side of the car. He's in the intensive care ward at Houston General Hospital. If any student has any information that could help the police discover who did this, I urge you to come forward. Policewoman Reynolds will be in my office all afternoon and you can talk to her."

The PA system shut off.

"Have you been interviewed yet?" Jean Marie asked Sophie.

"We all have. The principal waited until the police had seen everybody to make the announcement."

She thought of Mr. Jenks and the scene at the school bus. "Did you tell them what happened yesterday? About the argument with Cory?"

"Beating somebody over the head with a tire tool seems a bit much even for Cory. Mr. Jenks was just following the rules. Mrs. Adams was there, too, and she took charge."

"Yesterday, after you got on the bus, Cory told Mr. Jenks he'd remember this. Mr. Jenks called him a pissant."

"That would make Cory mad. Did anybody else hear them argue?"

"Mrs. Adams did."

"Did Cory get mad at her?"

"I don't think so. She was polite. She said school regulations required kids to go home on the bus or with parents, nobody else. Sophie, I think we should tell the police about the argument."

Sophie said, "We can't let Cory know we talked to the police. If he'd do that to Mr. Jenks, what do you think he'd do to somebody that reported him to the police?"

"I bet Mrs. Adams told them," Jean Marie said.

"You're right," Sophie said. "She must have told them."

Sophie looked relieved.

The bell rang, and they gathered their books for the next class.

"See you at lunch," Jean Marie said.

Jean Marie went through the cafeteria line and joined Sophie at their table. Sophie had a salad and a piece of chocolate cake.

"Dieting?" Jean Marie said when she sat down.

"Halfway." Sophie grinned. "Everybody knows if you have a salad for lunch you lose weight."

"What about the cake?"

79

"Everybody also knows that lettuce leaves scamper around sucking up spare calories, so the chocolate cake is okay."

"Have you thought any more about Cory and Mr. Jenks?" Jean Marie asked.

"I don't know what to do. If the police can't prove he did it, he's going to be really mad. I'm afraid of him, and I think my mother is, too."

Sophie played with her chocolate cake. She said, "Usually, my mother's not afraid of anybody. But Cory's different. Still, she told me not to worry, she'd take care of things."

"Your mother is a very tough lady."

"Mr. Jenks was even tougher."

They finished eating and went outside. They went to the far corner of the playground and sat on the grass under a live oak tree.

"How's Stephen?" Sophie asked.

"Stephen's father's not dead," Jean Marie said. She told Sophie about the scene with Stephen's father.

"I like Jeannette a lot more. You know, in her time, kids went to work when they were fourteen. She's been worried about what's going to happen to her when she leaves the hospital. Stephen's father told her he and Matron had it all arranged. She's going to someplace in the country with Matron's sister, and then she's going to school."

"What happens if what you saw is true? What if it happens later? What happens if Stephen's father dies?"

"Maybe Mr. Finkelstein won't die. Maybe it was a possibility, something that didn't have to happen."

"I don't think we can change the past," Sophie said.

"We've already changed it. The talk between Stephen's dad and Jeannette wouldn't have happened without the link between me and Jeannette."

"That was minor. You didn't influence what Mr. Finkelstein planned to do. He and the nurse were worried about Jeannette on their own. Sooner or later, they would have had the same talk."

"Maybe Mr. Finkelstein will be more careful," Jean Marie said, "and he won't get killed."

"He sounds careful anyway, without any warning from Jeannette," Sophie said. "If this is reincarnation, I think Stephen must be right. Jeannette has to be dead if you and she are the same people. Anybody you can identify as the same in both times must be dead as well."

"Jeannette, or anybody else, could die a long time after the time I'm seeing. There are years and years between 1940 and 1992, when I was born."

"True," Sophie said. "That would work."

"One other thing. At the bus, I heard Jeannette or I thought it, I don't know which. Somebody in my head thought 'Uncle Richard is back.' I knew, or Jeannette knew and told me, that her Uncle Richard was your mother's Cory."

"Uncle Richard is Jeannette's uncle?"

"Yeah. He was some sort of gangster. She's afraid of him."

"More research. He sounds like the kind that might get into the papers. If he's anything like Cory, they hanged him."

***

The air raid sirens sounding the all-clear in London blurred with the bell announcing the end of Jean Marie's lunch in Houston. For a moment, Jeannette was confused about where she was. She yawned and wondered what time it was. At home, she hadn't needed a clock. She could look out the window and tell the time from the way the sky looked and the sounds from the street.

With the blackout, she couldn't see the sky. There were no street sounds. In the hospital, she knew it was before 6 a.m. because the desk in the hall where Matron sat was dimly lit. At 6 a.m., all the lights in the hall went on and the hospital started work. Except for the last few days, when it seemed like work was constant. Matron and some of the other staff had given up trying to get home. Those without families slept on cots in the Staff Room.

She was hungry. Stephen had some biscuits on the table between them. She felt very virtuous. *I'm no thief. Besides, I'm mad at him still.*

Stephen had come back after his physio yesterday and ignored her. He had sat reading his book. She had worked on her homework, then knitted. Matron had taught her to knit. Stephen had been snarky.

"That looks like vomit," he said. "Grey vomit."

"It's for the war effort," she said. "You don't want pastel colors for the war effort."

"Making wads of grey stuff to clean the cannon?" he'd asked.

"It's socks for the troops," she said.

Then he'd gone back to his book and she'd gone back to knitting. She was irritated at Stephen and would not eat his biscuits. Then she heard him whisper.

"Psst…Jeannette, you awake?" Stephen said.

"Yes."

"Want some biscuits? It's a long time until breakfast."

"What time is it?"

Stephen was proud of his watch. The numbers were painted with mercury and glowed in the dark. He liked being asked the time.

"Zero-four-forty-five."

Jeannette smiled in the dark. Since Franz had come, Stephen used the 24-hour military clock.

Stephen told her it was simple. After noon, subtract twelve to get the time she was used to. She noticed if she dropped the teen and twenty business, and subtracted two, she got the right result and it was easier.

"So, want a biscuit?" Stephen asked again.

"Yes, please," she said.

Stephen was acting like nothing happened. He'd spent the afternoon sulking. She wasn't going to spend any more time sulking, herself. *Enough sulking,* she thought. *It's too much trouble to stay mad at Stephen. Besides, there's nobody else to talk to. He's like an older brother, a tedious older brother that is more trouble than he's worth, but I'm still very fond of him.*

Stephen handed her four biscuits. Custard cream, her favorite.

"When I was a child," Stephen said, "I used to take them apart and lick out the filling first. My brother used to whack me and say that was disgusting."

"There's a place in the East End where you can buy broken biscuits," Jeannette said. "Uncle Frank used to pick up a bag, a big bag, for a penny. He'd bring them round when he visited my Nan."

"We used to get those, too."

"I never liked the strawberry creams. Didn't taste like strawberries."

"I didn't either, but I like the plain and the chocolate."

Uncle Frank. Jeannette whispered, "Oh, no."

"What is it?" Stephen asked.

"Nothing."

"Come on, Jeannie-beanie. You gasp and say oh no and then tell me it's nothing? Dreams again? About my father?"

"Dreams, yes. About your father, no."

"Go ahead, then. What's happened?"

Jeannette told him about Cory and the argument when Cory came to pick up Sophie at school. Then she told him about the attack on Mr. Jenks.

"I knew Cory. I knew Mr. Jenks," she said. "I feel like everybody I know is in two places. Cory is my very unpleasant uncle here, today. Everybody but my Nan is afraid of him. My Nan and my Uncle Frank. Uncle Frank was there, too. I didn't recognize him right away because he was more different. Richard was still Richard, but Uncle Frank changed."

"How?"

"He was happier." Jeannette thought about it. "Uncle Frank was always working. He was on one of the teams on the dock, and he worked as many hours as he needed to unload cargo. When there wasn't work at the dock, he did other work. He turned his hand to anything going. My aunt, his wife, now she was a proper cow. Nagging, always wanting more than she had. In the future time, Mr. Jenks was a happy Uncle Frank. He was in the American Air Force, and he'd retired. He was still pretty young, so I'm glad in that life he had something more than work."

"How can you be sure it was your Uncle Frank?"

"Because of the way the Cory person acted. And the way Mr. Jenks acted. They hated each other on sight. Cory was like a snake, Mr. Jenks like a mongoose. Richard and Frank, they hated each other, too. My Nan refused to believe it but everybody else in the family knew. What happened at Sophie's bus, it was like some Christmases I remember. If my Nan hadn't been there, one of them would have killed the other."

She fell silent waiting for Stephen to say something. *I won't argue with him. I'll let it go, and ignore it, and go back to sleep. Poor Uncle Frank.* But Jeannette was proud of him. He'd looked like he'd done well in that future life.

"What is it exactly that you recognize?"

Jeannette thought about it. She said, "The bodies are different, and the names, and a lot of times the way people act. Imagine eggs. You can have them boiled or fried or scrambled in butter. They're still eggs. But if they're in a cake, I don't know if I'd recognize them. Uncle Richard was a boiled egg, easy to recognize. Uncle Frank was more like scrambled eggs."

"Let's assume you're right. Why are you having dreams and not me?"

"I don't know. The people there in the future, they're the people that are important to me now. I suppose you think this means I'm just fantasizing, my imagination making up a future that's really about my present."

"I don't know, Jeannette. My father was right about one thing. I can't explain it. Telepathy, reincarnation, precognition. Maybe it really is a connection with the future or parallel universes. However, my father is not going to die. That was just something you worried about. A bad dream, like my father said. Understood?"

"Understood. Jean Marie agrees with you. She doesn't think your father's going to die."

Stephen said. "We saw my father and he is very much all right. He's going to continue to be all right for a long, long time."

Chapter Nine

It was almost eight when Jean Marie shut down her computer. She'd been working ever since she got home, and her mother had just told her dinner was ready. *Homework is actually a nice distraction. Better than worrying about Sophie or Jeannette.*

The telephone rang, and Jean Marie answered. It was Sophie.

"You're allowed to use the phone again?"

"Cory and my mother went out to dinner. I think my mother wants to talk to him without me hearing. You hear everything in a trailer."

Jean Marie called to her mother, "Be right there, Mom. Sophie's on the phone." Then she said to Sophie, "What's up? We're about to eat."

"Somebody told the police about the argument between Cory and Mr. Jenks. Mrs. Henderson next door told me that the police came by today and talked to her. They wanted to know if she'd heard Cory leave the house last night. She told them she was as deaf as a post and wouldn't hear anything if there was anything to hear. She said they talked to Cory as well."

"Did you hear anything that night?"

"No. Then, Cory started questioning me as soon as I opened the front door. What did Mrs. Henderson want? Did the police question me at school? What did I say? He kept it up until my mother got home. My mother walked in, said she and Cory were going out to eat. She gave me money to get a pizza delivered, which I am eating now."

"The best thing that could happen would be for the police to arrest Cory," Jean Marie said.

"If he did it."

"If he didn't do that, he did something else."

"Dangerous thinking, Jean Marie. Arrest people for what they did, and what you can prove they did."

Jean Marie's mother called her again.

"I've got to go, time for dinner. I'll call you back."

"That's OK. I'm going to bed as soon as I finish eating. I'm tired. I've been having trouble sleeping and I'm going into my room, shutting the door, and sleeping for twelve hours. I'll see you at school tomorrow."

"Jean Marie, your food's getting cold. Tell Sophie you'll call her back."

"I'm coming," she called.

Jean Marie sat down at the table. Mashed potatoes, peas, pork chops.

"You didn't make any gravy," she grumbled.

She put some food on her plate and sat looking at it. Then she made a mountain of mashed potatoes, put peas on top, poked it with her fork. She was aware that her mother was irritated.

"I know," Jean Marie said, "if I didn't eat junk food all afternoon I'd be hungry and eat a good dinner."

"All right," her mother snapped, "you know it. Good. Either eat your food or don't. But please don't make a disgusting mess on your plate."

Jean Marie ate the pork chop, some mashed potatoes, and ignored the peas. Then she started to count them. One pea, two pea, three pea, four.

"God give me strength," her mother muttered.

Jean Marie laughed. "I really don't like peas."

"Then why did you put them on your plate?"

"If I hadn't, you would have told me to take a small spoonful and eat two bites." Jean Marie ate one pea. Then she ate another. "See? Two bites. I'm finished and I'll put my plate in the dishwasher."

After Jean Marie left the table, she went into the living room and turned on the television. She flipped through the different channels and turned off the TV. She went into her bedroom, picked up a book, and threw it down. She went back into the living room. Her mother was sitting on the sofa.

"Mother," she said. "Can I lend Sophie my cell phone tomorrow? For emergencies?"

Her mother turned off the television and said, "Are you expecting Sophie to have emergencies?"

"She might. I don't know."

"What kind of emergencies?"

"I'm not asking so Sophie and I can talk on the phone. There're only about three minutes left on the prepaid card, but that's enough to call 911 if she needs to."

"Does this have anything to do with Mr. Jenks? If you or Sophie know anything, you should tell the police."

"We don't know anything."

Jean Marie's mother looked at her watch. "It's 9:10 and the mall is still open. Come on, we'll drive over and get Sophie a cheap cell phone with a ten dollar prepaid card."

Jean Marie sat in the car as her mother drove to the mall. It was easier to explain in the dark.

"The police talked to Cory, the boyfriend, today. I think he attacked Mr. Jenks. Sophie doesn't. At least, Sophie thinks there is no evidence that he did. I don't have any evidence, either, but I think he could kill someone. Sophie's afraid of him. I want her to be able to call the police if she needs to."

Her mother said, "A good reason for a cell phone. I stop by Sophie's mother's diner some mornings for coffee. I'll stop by tomorrow, and if she wants to talk, I'll give her a chance. That's all we can do."

The next day, Mrs. Semak, her homeroom teacher, told her to report to the principal's office. The policewoman and the principal were waiting for her. She noticed another policeman with a video camera.

"Come in, Jean Marie," the principal said. "Sit down. Officer Reynolds has a few questions to ask you."

"Yes, sir." Jean Marie sat down.

"Jean Marie, do you remember a scene outside Mr. Jenks' s bus the day he was attacked?"

"Yes, ma'am."

"Can you tell me about it?"

"Cory, my friend Sophie's mother's boyfriend, came to pick her up after school."

Officer Reynolds interrupted Jean Marie, "Did Sophie want to go with Cory?"

"No." Jean Marie continued. "Mr. Jenks told him it was against school regulations, and Sophie had to ride the bus home. Then Mrs. Adams came over and said the same thing. Sophie got on the bus. Cory was mad."

"Did he say anything to Mr. Jenks?"

"He told him he'd remember this. Mr. Jenks said he could remember all he wanted to, he wasn't a little girl that could be scared. He called Cory a pissant. Then Cory left, got in his car, and drove off."

"Did Mr. Jenks say anything else?"

"Yes. I said I was scared and he said I shouldn't be. The man was just a pissant to be stepped on."

Jean Marie sat silently, waiting for more questions.

"Has Sophie told you she heard Cory leave the trailer that night?"

Jean Marie wondered what Sophie had said.

"No," she said.

"Do you think Sophie might have heard something, and be afraid to tell us?

"No. Sophie doesn't tell lies. Ever. Whatever she told you is true. I've spent the night with her, and she sleeps very soundly. If somebody creeped out, she wouldn't wake up."

"But she might wake up if a car started."

"Maybe. But the park is a couple of blocks from Sophie's house. If somebody cut through the park, Mr. Jenks' house is right there, facing the park. Cory wouldn't need to use his car."

The policeman turned off the video camera. The interview seemed to be over.

Jean Marie said, "I know it's not evidence or proof, but Cory looked at Mr. Jenks like he hated him. When he said he'd remember this, it was a threat."

"Thank you, Jean Marie," the principal said. "Miss Willis will give you a note to give your teacher so you won't be marked tardy."

Jean Marie had a minute before her history class began to talk to Sophie. "I saw the police this morning." she said. "They asked me about the bus thing."

"I saw them last night," Sophie said. "Right after we hung up. I think they were watching the trailer and saw my mom and Cory leave. They asked me if he'd gone out that night, and I said I didn't know. I was asleep, but I'd probably wake up if he left the trailer."

"Dumb," Jean Marie said. "Dumb, dumb, dumb. You don't have to lie, but you don't have to support his alibi either. You don't know whether he left or not."

"There's more, but it's too complicated to tell you now. It's almost time for the bell."

Jean Marie went back to her seat.

At lunchtime, she joined Sophie at their table. She handed her the cell phone.

"Here. It's got ten dollars worth of calls prepaid. You might need it."

Sophie took the phone. "Thank you. How much did it cost? I'll pay you back."

"It's a gift. You can't pay me for it. I'll be insulted. Besides, my mom bought it."

"I hope I don't need it. Thanks again and thank your mom for me."

The two ate quickly and left the school cafeteria. A cold north wind was blowing and the temperature had fallen since that morning. The sky was gray and it looked like it was going to rain. They went to the wild oak and sat under its branches. It made a good windbreak, and Jean Marie almost felt warm.

"This is cozy," Jean Marie said.

"It's almost Christmas. It's getting too cold and wet to come outside. But you're right, it's nice under the tree branches."

Jean Marie leaned back against the tree trunk and waited for Sophie to begin.

Sophie said, "Last night, when my mother and Cory got home, I heard them talking. Cory said he loved my mother and he wasn't leaving. My mother said she loved him, too, but he had to go. She said, 'I'm afraid of you, Cory. I'm afraid you'll hurt me or my daughter. I won't risk it. You can stay until after the weekend. Then, I expect you to leave. I'll help you find a place, and I'll see if I can get an advance on my salary to help you pay your first month's rent on an apartment. But you've got to go, Cory.'"

"What did he say?"

"He said she was upset about this business with the bus driver. They'd talk about it tomorrow. Then they went to bed."

"You think he'll leave?"

"He'll have to be pried out with a crowbar. He doesn't want to go, but he sounded calm. He thinks he can talk my mother 'round."

"That was clever of your mother to tell him she loved him."

"Oh, Jean Marie! That wasn't clever. She does love him. She's terrified of him, she's afraid he's going to hurt her or me, and she still loves him."

Jean Marie said, "Your mother has serious problems, psychological problems."

"That's a useless, garbage thing to say!"

"I didn't say she was crazy, just she had a problem."

"Phrasing the matter like that doesn't suggest a solution, except maybe to send her to a shrink. She wouldn't go and we can't afford a shrink if she would."

"Have you thought about leaving? I'm pretty sure my mom would let you stay with us." Jean Marie thought a minute. "She kept a totally psychotic dog for three months. Somebody she didn't even like lost their apartment because of the dog. She kept him until the woman found a new place. The dog took over the living room and snapped if you wanted his chair."

"I'm sure my teeth are smaller. Thanks for the comparison, J.M."

"I didn't mean it like that."

"Sophie and a psychotic dog, relying on the kindness of others. Thank your mother for the cell phone. Thank you again for thinking of it. My crazy mother and I are very, very grateful."

Sophie got up and walked towards the cafeteria. Jean Marie watched her leave. *Sophie knows I don't think she's a psychotic dog. She knows I don't think her mother is crazy. What's she on about? She's acting like a total idiot. At least she took the phone.* Jean Marie decided to look for Sophie at the buses. *Or maybe I won't. Maybe I'll wait for her to apologize.* Reluctantly, Jean Marie decided that was a stupid thing to do. *One of us has to be sensible. There's only room for one prima donna at a time. I suppose it's Sophie's turn.*

When Jean Marie looked for Sophie after school, she couldn't find her. Somebody said her mother had picked her up.

***

Stephen was exhausted after his physiotherapy session. Jeannette waited for him to start talking. Strange. He was much more calm and even-tempered before he started getting better. He never used to yell. The last few days had been nothing but Stephen being snarky.

She went on answering the questions in her math worksheet.

"I can handle the flat on crutches," Stephen said, "but I don't think I'll ever be able to climb stairs."

"How important is your dignity?" Jeannette asked.

"I don't care about that."

"You could sit on a step, boost yourself to the next with your arms and good leg, and drag the bad leg behind you."

"I'd rather die."

"It's undignified, but I think it would work."

"I'd rather die," Stephen repeated.

"Would you rather stay in the hospital or go back to school? You missed dying nine months ago," Jeannette continued. "Paul thinks you'll get the hang of climbing stairs."

"Paul's not the one doing it."

For a moment, Jeannette felt bitter. Stephen was leaving with a brace on one leg and crutches. Paul thought Stephen could manage. "Functional mobility", Paul said. Jeannette had braces on both legs and hadn't even tried to walk yet. Her physiotherapy sessions were spent in the pool. At least she'd learned to swim. One of the best things about the water was getting the heavy, clunky braces off.

After a minute, Stephen said, "Sorry, Jeannie. I'm supposed to go back to school in two months. I'm not sure I'll be ready."

"You'll be ready," Jeannette said. "You've worked at getting ready ever since you got here."

"It wasn't so bad before the school was evacuated."

"If the school hadn't been evacuated, you'd take buses or the underground to school. At least this way you live next to your classes."

"Everybody's going to stare," Stephen said abruptly. "I'll always be Stephen the cripple. I hate it when people feel sorry for me."

"They'll stare at first," Jeannette said. "They'll get used to the crutch. You told me when I first came in here that the hot wraps and the stretching were temporary. The pain was temporary. I had to put up with it if I wanted to walk again. You told me to stop whining."

"So now I should stop whining."

"Whine all you want to. Don't get discouraged and stop working, though."

They heard the trollies in the hall. Lunchtime. The orderly brought them their trays.

"Steamed fish, boiled potatoes, and cabbage," Stephen said, taking the cover off his plate.

"I could tell that from the smell in the hall," Jeannette said.

"It could be worse. It could be liver and onions."

"I like liver and onions."

"Is there any food you don't like, Jeannette?"

"Marrows. I don't like marrows very much, but what difference does that make? You eat what's on the plate, and nobody cares whether you like it or not. Eat it fast, don't chew, just let it slide down."

"A full tummy and a nice nap," Jeannette said after she finished eating.

"A nice nap …I've been having dreams, Jeannette. Dreams where I'm really scared and I don't know why. I know there's something threatening me and my family. I'm afraid of someone. I'm small, I'm weak and I'm helpless. I have to protect somebody, and I can't.

It's like an Agatha Christie mystery. One person's dead and it's not over."

Sophie, Jeannette thought. "Can you remember anything at all about the dreams?"

"Just what I feel and something about the situation. I suppose my father's right, and everybody's having bad dreams. I don't want to remember them. I want them to go away."

"They could be like my dreams," Jeannette said.

"Your future sounds exciting. This is grim. If I'm dreaming about the future, I'd rather stay in the present, bombs and all."

Stephen took a drink of water. He said, "Last night was worst of all. Something very bad happened, something I'd been afraid of. I don't want to remember it."

Jeannette heard footsteps in the hall, three sets of footsteps. I've heard this before.

She saw Matron, Paul, and a policeman standing in the doorway.

Matron said, "Jeannette, Paul has time to give you an extra physiotherapy session."

Jeannette sat up and Paul helped her into a wheelchair. As she was wheeled from the room, she heard Stephen say, "Something's happened, Matron."

Chapter Ten

Jean Marie was doing stretching exercises when her mother came in. She stopped, surprised.

"You're home early," she said.

"Sophie's mother called me today. We met for coffee, and I just left her."

"What did she have to say?"

"She's in the middle of a situation. We talked about it, and Sophie's going to spend a week or so here. She's going to bring Sophie over tonight. Go straighten your bedroom up."

Jean Marie went into her bedroom and straightened her desk. She picked up books and papers scattered on the floor next to the bed. She made the bed and vacuumed her floor, then the hall, then the living room.

Her mother was surprised.

"As long as I have it out," Jean Marie said, "might as well do it all."

She was putting the vacuum cleaner away when she heard a car drive up, the car door slam, and then the front doorbell rang.

Jean Marie opened the door. Sophie stood there with a suitcase.

"Hi," Jean Marie said awkwardly. "I looked for you after school."

"My mother picked me up about two. She wanted to pick up my clothes and stuff while Cory was gone."

"Probably a good idea," Jean Marie said.

Sophie came in and put her overnight bag down in the hall. "Sorry I went off in a huff. I do appreciate the phone."

"Forget the phone," Jean Marie said. "Forget today at lunch. I'm glad you're here."

"I didn't want to leave my mother. She said I had to leave. Mom said I was a hostage, that it would be more difficult for her if I was there. She'd be worrying about me. So, I agreed to come."

Sophie walked into the kitchen and said to Jean Marie's mother, "Thank you for the cell phone for emergencies. Thank you for asking me over."

"That's quite all right, Sophie. I was at the mall and noticed the phones on sale. I remembered you didn't have one. I think every teenager should have one, in case of emergencies."

Mrs. Hastings was standing at the sink, washing carrots.

"Can I help you with that?" Sophie asked.

"We're having beef stew tonight. I like beef stew and usually don't get home early enough to make it. You can chop the carrots after I wash them."

"What can I do?" Jean Marie said.

"The beef's already on so we just need to add the vegetables. You have the choice between chopping onions or peeling potatoes."

"I'll take the potatoes."

Mrs. Hastings put the prepared vegetables into the simmering beef and added some tomatoes, thyme, parsley, and a bay leaf. She joined the girls at the table.

The doorbell rang. Mrs. Hastings went to answer it. When she opened the door, she saw Cory. He stepped inside but he didn't shut the front door.

"I just stopped by to tell Sophie something," Cory said, "to reassure her."

Sophie came into the hall.

"I found the little toe-rag that took your computer and printer, Sophie. I got them back for you. I knew you were worried."

"Thank you," Sophie said.

"No problem," he said. "You are important to your mother. Your mother is important to me."

Cory acted like there was no one in the hall but Sophie. *He doesn't see anything he doesn't want to,* Jean Marie thought. *He knows what he wants, and that's all that's important.*

"You and I are going to have to deal, Sophie. One way or the other, we'll reach an accommodation."

He's talking to Sophie like she's a grown-up, some kind of competition for Sophie's mother that he's sure he'll win.

"I don't think I appreciated that in the beginning," Cory said. "A fine woman, like your mother, she's going to be responsible, take care of her child. She's going to see how I make it easier."

Sophie said, "I think I didn't understand some things in the beginning as well."

"You thought I needed a place to stay, was taking financial advantage of your momma," Cory laughed and seemed to be genuinely amused. "I've always got a place to stay. I don't need your momma's support."

"I believe you," Sophie said. "But I don't believe you'll make my mother happy."

"You'll just have to let me prove you wrong." Cory turned around went out and shut the door behind him. Jean Marie, Sophie, and Mrs. Hastings stood in the hall until they heard Cory's car start and drive away.

"So," Mrs. Hastings said, "that's the boyfriend."

"That's Cory," Sophie said.

"I wish he didn't know where we lived," Jean Marie said.

They went back to the kitchen table and sat down.

"So, that's the boyfriend," Mrs. Hastings said again. "I understand better what your mother was talking about when I saw her this morning."

Mrs. Hastings got three bowls out of the cupboard and put stew in them. She brought the food to the table.

"Sophie," Mrs. Hastings said, "Your mother is one of the most competent people I know. She manages the diner with six waitresses and two cooks. She plans the menus and does all the ordering. What she does isn't easy, and she's good at it. Your mother can take care of herself."

Jean Marie said, "If Sophie's mother is so competent, why did she get involved with such a loser in the first place?"

"You say he's a loser because you're afraid of him," Sophie said. "It makes him sound easier to manage. I did the same thing. But he's not just a loser."

Mrs. Hastings said. "We must be careful not to underestimate Cory."

They went in and sat down in front of the TV. They heard a bleep from Jean Marie's mother's computer.

"A Skype call from my sister in Geneva," Mrs. Hastings said, delighted. "I'm glad you're here, Sophie. I've told her about you."

They crowded in front of the computer, and a smiling, middle-aged woman came on the screen.

It's Dr. Baron, Jean Marie thought. *Dr. Baron, that Stephen and Jeannette liked so much, that everybody liked. The one she thought her Uncle Richard killed.*

"Sarah," Mrs. Hastings said. "How's Geneva?"

"Nice as always, but cold. So, this is Sophie. I've been wanting to meet you."

"What do you do in Geneva?" Sophia asked.

"I'm an epidemiologist, watching out for possible epidemics, planning."

"That sounds like a neat job. Puzzles to solve plus helping people. Best job around."

"I think so."

Jean Marie hesitated, then thought, then told her aunt of her dreams, of England in WWII, of the people that kept coming up, in a pattern. "And you were one of them," she said. "Dr. Baron, and she helped everybody until somebody murdered her."

"To quote, or paraphrase, Hamlet, 'There are more things in Heaven and Earth, Horatio, than are dreamt of in your philosophy'. To paraphrase somebody else, if it quacks like a duck, waddles like a duck, swims like a duck, it's a duck. From what you've said, I think running is in order. This Cory is hard news. Maybe one reason you're having these dreams is to give you a chance to get away. Sophie, you and your mother should run. Just drive away."

***

After her time in the pool, Marie, Paul's assistant, helped her dress. Jeannette looked at herself in the mirror. Her hair was cut short, like a boy's. It was much easier to handle. Marie toweled it dry, combed it, and was finished.

I look like a rat, she thought. *A rat just out of a flooded drain sewer.*

When Marie laughed, Jeannette realized she'd said it aloud.

"If you were a rat from a sewer, you'd be dirty. You're all clean, Jeannette."

Marie opened her handbag and took out a small bottle. Opened it and put a small dab of liquid on Jeannette's wrist. "Smell that."

Jeannette smelled lavender and she remembered her Nan ironing. Her Nan put blueing in the rinse water after she washed white things and hung them to dry. When they were almost dry, her Nan took them down from the line and got out the ironing board. She sprinkled them with water with a little lavender in it, and the hot iron going over the clothes made a smell like this.

"It's been a long time since I've smelled anything but hospital smells," Jeannette said. She sniffed her wrist again.

"I wish I could see something besides hospital walls. I wish I could see outside."

"Why not?" Paul said. He slid Jeannette into the wheelchair and took several large towels from the stack. He wrapped one around her wet hair, another around her shoulders.

Paul wheeled her to the elevator and they got in. He punched the highest button and the elevator went up. When the elevator door slid open, Jeannette saw the outside.

Paul wheeled her out onto the roof. The sky was very blue. There were no clouds. A small, three-sided shed had been set up in the middle of the roof. *The fire watchers must sit there when it rains*, Jeannette thought.

"When they built the extension to the hospital," Paul said, "they gave it a flat roof. I think there was some idea that patients could come up here and sit in the sun. We've never used it for that, but this is where we watch for fires."

"What about the old, slanted roof?"

"The pitch isn't bad. We've had one incendiary bomb hit it. We climbed on the roof and put it out with sand."

"Can I look over the side?"

Paul wheeled her to the edge of the roof. A low wall ran around the edge. She looked out over London.

"Over there, it's a clear day and you can see St. Paul's Cathedral. There's Westminster Abbey."

"The Thames. There's the river, running through the city."

Paul left her and went to the shed. She turned and watched him light a Bunsen burner and put a flask of water on to boil. She felt the sun and wind on her face and looked out. Paul brought her a cup of tea.

"We're looking west." she said. "Can I see east?"

"The main hospital building is in the way."

"That damage, there, from bombs. Where's that?"

"The City of Westminster."

"Stephen's father's dead, isn't he?"

"Yes."

Paul waited for her to ask more questions. Finally, Jeannette said, "I'm tired of hearing how people died. They were alive, now they're dead. I'm going to miss Mr. Finkelstein very much. I don't think there's any point in talking about it."

"No," Paul agreed, "there's not."

"Can I stay up here awhile? Sit in the sun? I'll be all right alone."

"Thirty minutes," Paul said. "I've got some paperwork to do, and I'll leave you for thirty minutes."

He adjusted the wheelchair and locked the wheels. "Don't try to move around," he warned.

Jeannette heard the elevator come up, the doors open, close, then the elevator descended.

"I'm by myself for the first time in a year," she said aloud.

When someone died, everyone came round. They came with food, usually. They talked and they chattered away about nothing. You were never supposed to let someone grieving be on their own. She thought Stephen would prefer some time, at least, with no one else in the room.

Jeannette started to sing. She sang an old song, one her Nan had sung. So many people had died.

She cried.

By the time Paul returned, she was done crying.

Stephen was sitting up in his bed when Paul wheeled her back to the room. Paul helped her to bed. After he left the room, she said, "I'm sorry."

Stephen didn't answer.

Jeannette tried to think of something to say. Had anyone said anything that made her feel better when her Nan died? Heaven? A better place? No more pain and suffering. She decided that none of these were very comforting. She kept quiet.

For the first time, Stephen didn't turn on his little radio to listen to the news. He lay in bed and pretended to sleep. After a while, Jeannette fell asleep. For the first time in weeks, the air raid sirens didn't go off. London had a peaceful night.

The next morning, while they were eating breakfast, Stephen spoke to her for the first time. "Why," he asked, "did we have the warning when we could do nothing about it? What good was it?"

"I don't know, Stephen."

"I should have been able to prevent it. You told me, and I should have found out more. I'm supposed to be so clever."

He's remembering what he said to his father, Jeannette thought.

"Clever clogs, Stephen. I sat here and told him he was ignorant, not to talk about things he didn't understand. I said that after all the work he did so I could get an education."

"He wasn't upset, Stephen. After you left the room, he laughed. He said you always acted angry when you were afraid. He said you were afraid he was going to die, that's why you said those things."

"I said them. It was unforgivable to say things like that."

Jeannette tried again. "Your father understood. He was proud of you. He said parents always wanted their children to be better than they were."

"I'm certainly not ever going to be better than my father."

"Probably not. He was a very good man. You can try. Your father would expect you to try."

Stephen didn't answer her. After a few minutes, Jeannette picked up her library book. Treasure Island. Mr.

103

Finkelstein had checked it out of the library on his ticket and brought it to her. Who would take it back? She'd have to ask Paul. *Such a stupid thing to be thinking about,* she thought. She tried to concentrate on the book.

"Good morning."

Jeannette looked up from her book, Stephen sat up and opened his eyes.

A large woman wearing a fur coat walked into the room. She adjusted her glasses and looked at the chart on the foot of Stephen's bed.

"Stephen Finkelstein," she said. "I thought you must be he. Only two children left in the hospital, well, I've found you."

It's too hot to wear fur. Yesterday was almost like spring. She's wearing it to show she's got it Jeannette thought.

"Now what are we going to do with you, Stephen?"

Jeannette waited for Stephen to say something. He remained silent.

"Who," Jeannette asked, "are you?"

The woman frowned. "I'm Mrs. Reynolds, the volunteer social worker. I've come to tell Stephen the arrangements I've made. He must be worried about the future."

Volunteer Social Worker. A do-gooder, knows what's best for everyone. Especially those with no money. My Nan never liked those people.

"You're doing well. The doctors think you should be mobile soon. It says here that your father was a tailor. That's fortunate. There is no reason a cripple cannot be a tailor. You sew with your hands, after all, not your feet." The woman tittered.

Stephen simply looked at her.

She went on, "I don't know why you children have been left here. You should have been shifted a month ago. At any rate, Stephen, I can arrange for you to be

104

shifted to a youth shelter for the homeless until you can be apprenticed to a tailor. Your father was employed at a good establishment on Saville Row. Perhaps as a matter of sentiment, they might take you on."

Jeannette waited for Stephen to object. He said nothing.

"Miss," she said, "Stephen's got a scholarship. He's going to school. The Headmaster's kept his place. It's in the country, and he's going after Christmas."

"Mrs. Reynolds," the woman corrected her. "That was in the past. The boy may have a scholarship, but he's an orphan now, the ward of the city of London. I can't allow him to go to some strange school."

"It's not a strange school," Jeannette said. "It's a London school, been evacuated to the country. Half of London's children are evacuated to the country."

"He may have a scholarship, but there're other expenses. Books, uniforms. The ratepayer can't be expected to pay for that."

"It's cheaper," Jeannette said. "You'll have to pay for his lodgings and his food. If he goes to school, that's paid for.

"Who are you?" the woman asked.

"Jeannette Bagg," Jeannette said.

"Oh, yes, I remember your file. You're the little girl abandoned by her family, the one that will never be able to walk."

"Yes, she will," Stephen said. "She'll walk."

Matron came to the door. "Mrs. Reynolds," she said, "what are you doing here?"

"I came to tell the boy what was going to happen to him."

Matron said. "I believe Mr. Finkelstein, Stephen's father, left a will with instructions and provision for Stephen's future."

"Nonsense. People like that don't make wills."

Matron seemed to expand. She was a large woman, but she became even larger. Her white uniform was always stiff and starched. Now it looked like Joan of Arc's armor.

"Mr. Finkelstein has made a will. Copies are left in his solicitor's office, Sir James Whaley, and, I assume, have been properly deposited in Somerset House."

Matron's voice could take on a certain tone that said you will do as you are told. Now, that voice curled, crisped, and flamed. The King Himself could only say, "Yes, Matron."

"Sir James Whaley?"

"Sir James Whaley."

A 'sir'. Hah! A 'sir' in front of a name is enough to shut the old cow up, Jeannette thought. *That should make sure Stephen isn't pushed into some shelter.*

"Matters are well in hand, Mrs. Reynolds."

Matron stood by the door, expecting the woman to leave.

"I shall do something about the other child."

"That has also been sorted," Matron said.

The woman left.

"Matron," Jeannette said, "you could sort Hitler by yourself."

Matron said. "I can certainly sort the likes of Mrs. Reynolds. Silly woman, prancing up to one of my patients. Your father made things a lot easier, Stephen. You would not end up in some shelter whatever happened. But your father did make a will several weeks ago. He named me and one of your tutors temporary guardians until your brother comes home."

"In a will prepared by Sir James Whaley?"

"Your father was Sir James' tailor. Sir James is also one of the volunteer fire wardens in Westminster. They were on watch one night and your father told him how worried he was about you, in case something happened. Sir James told him to come by his

Chambers the next morning. He made the will himself, professional courtesy, he said, one fire warden to another."

"I won't go to the Youth Shelter?"

"This is 1940, Stephen," Matron said. "One of the few good things to come out of this is the way we are getting to know each other. Sir James called on the telephone this morning. He's organised a memorial service for your father in Westminster. He wanted to know if you were mobile enough to go. I told him you could manage. He'll pick you up in his automobile."

After Matron left, Jeannette said, "She was like Joan of Arc."

"Boudica," Stephen said. "She was very English."

"She's Welsh."

"Maybe I should be a tailor, like my father. As the woman said, cripples can still sew," Stephen said.

"Your father didn't want to be a tailor. He was a good tailor because he'd work at anything he had to do. He wanted to be a librarian."

"A librarian?"

"He told me that one day."

"You knew he was going to die. Jean Marie told you, you told me, and it didn't make any difference."

"But it did make a difference," Jeannette said. "It gave your father a chance to make sure you were all right."

Chapter Eleven

Jean Marie and Sophie woke up at the same time. Jean Marie looked at the clock, and it was 6 a.m. She yawned and remembered what she had seen in her sleep. She told Sophie about the social worker visiting Stephen.

"Jeannette had it right. We couldn't prevent Mr. Finkelstein's death, but we did prevent Stephen from being sent to some sort of home." Jean Marie sounded triumphant.

"It looks as if we've changed the past," Sophie said. "Now the question is, have we changed the present?"

"That doesn't follow at all," Jean Marie said. "Mr. Finkelstein still died, nobody interfered with reincarnation. Wherever his soul went, it's still free to go there. Stephen's life is just better."

Sophie said, "You and Jeannette are connected. We know that. We also know that you are in different bodies at different times. We have two different states that are connected. Changes in one state should lead to changes in another."

"Changes in one state were for the better. If there are changes in our time, they should be for the better, too."

"I don't think quantum mechanics knows anything about better or worse. Just change."

"If there's no past, present and future, what happens is always what is supposed to happen," Jean Marie argued. "There's no way of changing anything. From the very beginning, I was supposed to dream about Stephen's father's death. There was no change."

"Only if the universe is deterministic, if everything is the result of laws that say when X happens, Y follows. What if the universe is probabilistic? Like throwing dice? Throw dice and a number one through six comes up. You stuck your little hand into the past, a new player joined the game, threw the dice and a new number came up."

"Whether change happened or not, I'm glad Stephen is doing what he wants to do."

They heard Mrs. Hastings go into her bathroom. Jean Marie said, "Flip a coin to see who gets my bathroom first?"

Sophie said, "Deterministic. There's a rule. Guests get the bathroom first."

She jumped out of bed and raced to the bathroom. Jean Marie stayed in bed laughing. She slipped into the hazy half-sleep where she could sometimes contact Jeannette. Slowly, she felt Jeannette's presence.

"Stephen okay?" she asked.

"He will be. Now, he's going on about how his father should have gone to Southampton instead of staying in London."

"Tell him it's a deterministic universe and that would have made no difference."

"What's a deterministic universe?"

"Only God and Sophie know, and probably Stephen. I don't. At least not well enough to tell you. But it might impress Stephen."

"What sort of mischief is Cory making?"

"That only Cory knows."

Sophie came back into the room, toweling her hair.

"I love your shower," she said. "Lots of hot water. All the hot water in the world. I hate cold showers."

Jeannette's presence disappeared. Jean Marie got up and went to take her own shower.

The rest of the week passed in a generalized fog of misery. Friday was surprisingly good. The girls got their report cards. Jean Marie had a mix of A's and B's, more

A's than B's. It was the best report card she had ever brought home. Her mother was amazed. Sophie, of course, expected all A's. She got one B. She laughed.

"I don't really care."

Mrs. Hastings took the girls out to dinner to celebrate.

Saturday morning, Mrs. Hastings said she didn't want to leave the girls at home alone.

"This is almost over," she said. She looked at Sophie and said, "Your mother called this morning. She thinks Cory is finally becoming more reasonable. She's taken off work this weekend, and they are looking at some apartments. But it's not over yet, and you two can come to the library with me."

When they got to the library, Sophie asked if she could look through the microfiche records from 1940 and 1941.

"We've finished with that in history," Jean Marie said. "We're already up to the Korean War."

"I know," Sophie said. "I'm just interested."

Mrs. Hastings brought back the boxes of spooled tape and Sophie threaded them and started looking at them.

After a while, Jean Marie noticed the disappearance of the click click click of the microfiche turning the film in the spools. She looked up. Sophie had turned off the machine and was leaning back in her chair.

"Bored?" Jean Marie asked.

"Bored? No, not bored," Sophie said.

"Did you find something?'

"Maybe."

"What?"

"I'm not sure you want to know. Does Jeannette know everything you do? Can you hide something from her?"

"I've never tried. Tell me why I want to."

"Change, change, Jean Marie." Sophie continued. "You think that Jeannette and you are the same people. You are a reincarnation of Jeannette. That means Jeannette is dead. What if I found something that gave a date for her death? What if you told her and the death was prevented? What would happen to you, Jean Marie?"

"I might not exist," Jean Marie said.

"Do you want to risk that?"

"If it were you, Sophie, what would you do? Would you say your life was more important than somebody else's? Would you warn whoever it was?"

"I don't know."

Jean Marie got up. "I'm going to get a Coke. See you in a minute."

Jean Marie left the library and sat on a bench outside drinking her Coke. She remembered the first time she felt Jeannette. She felt pain and heat and fear. She thought of how Jeannette had changed during the time she'd known her. She remembered Mr. Finkelstein saying it was a brave new world.

Jeannette didn't believe in brave new worlds. She was determined to face whatever world she had bravely. Jeannette wasn't expecting her life to improve. What did Jeannette have to look forward to anyway? Half the time, Jeannette was afraid she'd end up begging on the side of the street. Jean Marie remembered how happy Jeannette had been on top of the roof, just to sit in the sun and feel the wind.

If somebody threatened you, you had a right to defend yourself even if the other person died. Did you have a right to defend yourself even if that meant someone else, an innocent person, died? *Can I decide that Jeannette's life is not as good as mine? Can I let Jeannette die because I might, just might, not ever be born? That isn't self-defense. It's not murder, but it's not right, either.*

Jean Marie went back into the library

"Sophie, you said you wouldn't lie to get Cory arrested for Mr. Jenks's murder."

"No," Sophie said.

"You'd even give him an alibi if you honestly could."

"Yes," Sophie said.

"Somebody might pretend that getting Cory arrested is self-defense. It's not. It's not self-defense for me to ignore threats to Jeannette's life, either. I don't know what the stupid universe is going to do. The universe can do whatever it wants. I do know what I'm going to do. That's all I need to know. Tell me what you read, Sophie."

Sophie was silent.

"If I have to look through all that junk, I will," Jean Marie said.

"On December 14, 1940, bombs fall on the hospital. The new wing is completely destroyed. There wasn't a list of the dead, but the authorities say no one survived. In the next day's paper, I read that the dead were mainly hospitalized soldiers. There were only two children left in the children's hospital. They and some of the hospital staff were the other victims."

***

Stephen was still silent, still thinking about his father's death. He's treating guilt like a dog with a bone, Jeannette thought. Worrying it, turning it this way and that, chewing on it. Just how much is his fault?

Jeannette said, "Jean Marie said to tell you the universe was deterministic."

"Of course it is," he said impatiently. "And I also know they drink tea in China."

"She said it was important to remember. She said the universe isn't probable, probable something."

"It's not probable. It's actual."

"I've got the word wrong. It's the opposite of deterministic."

"Indeterminate?"

"No. Sounds like probable."

"Probabilistic," Stephen said. "Was that what she said?"

"Yes. Sophie thinks the universe is probabilistic."

"Nonsense. God doesn't play dice with the universe."

Well, that wasn't as much help as Jean Marie thought it would be. Jeannette thought.

"But I think I understand what Jean Marie and Sophie may mean. Jean Marie is saying that nothing that we did based on future information can change things. That is something you need to remember, Stephen," Jeannette said.

Jeannette had done the best she could. She ignored Stephen and read her book.

"Jeannette," Stephen said. "You're a good sort. I'm glad you're around. I know I've got to get on with things, but not yet."

They finished the day. They avoided discussing the next day, the day of Mr. Finkelstein's funeral. The woman who lived next door to Stephen's father brought Stephen's suit to the hospital. Matron pulled the curtain around his bed and helped him dress. When the curtain opened again, Stephen was standing by his bed, supported by his crutches.

He said, "My father must have let out the seam in the pant leg. It fits over the brace. I'm taller but thinner. I can still wear the suit. I think it looks all right. What do you think, Jeannette?"

"Very dashing, very handsome." Jeannette said. If you ignore the two-inch gap between the end of the sleeve and his hand, it is a good fit. But Stephen still looks very handsome. That must be the only thing Mr. Finkelstein didn't have time to do. "Your father would be proud."

When Stephen came back from his father's funeral, he sat down on the chair beside her bed.

"Jeannette, I'm leaving."

"Now?"

"After Christmas. Mr. Hartsill is spending a week in town. He's the teacher my father asked to be my temporary guardian. He came to London for the service for my father. He's coming to London for Christmas, and I'll take the train with him."

"Good," Jeannette said. "It's time for you to get on with your life. You've worked to leave the hospital, and you've done it."

"I'm worried about you, Jeannie-beanie. You'll be left here alone."

"I'm fine. Besides, you're going to write me."

"You have to write me back."

Stephen reached into his pocket and took out a silver pencil like the one his brother had given him. He handed her the pencil.

"Sir James gave me five pounds after the funeral. He said to buy something I didn't need but wanted. 'This five pounds,' he said, 'is only for a frivolous expenditure.'"

"Five pounds!"

"So I got you a pencil like mine."

Jeannette took the mechanical pencil. The silver looked soft and shiny. She turned the pencil around catching the light.

"Thank you very much, Stephen. Tell me all the rest of it. Your father's memorial service. Did many people come? What did they say about him?"

"There were a lot of people there, maybe a hundred. People came from the shop where my father worked. The owner gave an address." Stephen thought a minute. "It was good and it was funny. He said my father couldn't sew a crooked seam or walk a crooked mile if his life depended on it. He said my dad was straight clear through."

"Absolutely true," Jeannette said.

"Lord James talked, too. He talked about how brave my father was. Somebody from the Workers' Institute and Library came and talked about how my father loved books and learning. Then the Choir from the Institute sang Jerusalem. We went to the graveside, came back, and then there were tea and buns. Chelsea buns. There were a lot of flowers. Matron and Paul sent a wreath. Did you know? They put your name on it along with theirs."

"I'm glad. Did you bring back the tags on the flowers? You have to write thank you notes to everybody that sent flowers and everybody that came."

"I forgot about that. My father did that when my mother died. He used the Remembrance Book that everybody signed at the funeral. I did bring that back. I'll write thank you for coming and all you did. That covers flowers and anything else."

"You're a boy. They won't expect much better. That's a very good idea, Stephen."

"Tomorrow, Mr. Hartsill is coming by. He's going with me to the school's outfitters. I'll get measured for new uniforms."

"Yes."

Jeannette wanted to ask Stephen if he were still afraid of returning to school. Instead, she said, "I hope I see you in your new uniform."

"You will. The delivery boy from the outfitters is bringing them to the hospital the day before we leave in case something's not right."

"Good."

Stephen pulled the curtain between their beds and started to change. She heard his voice, slightly muffled from behind the curtain.

115

"Do you realize," Stephen said, "that this is the first time I've dressed and undressed by myself in a year and a half? This morning, Matron helped me but she's off somewhere with Mr. Hartsill. There's a little money. Not much, but enough. My father saved a few bob every week in a postal account. He took some out when my mother was sick. Some more because of me getting sick."

Jeannette turned her back on him, pulled her blanket over her head, and tried not to cry. Stephen took a long time. By the time he opened the curtain, Jeannette was ready to sit up and read her book.

Stephen looked like he might have been crying as well.

"For his old age," Stephen said. "He'd put some money by for his old age. In the will, he said it was for my education."

"That's a good use for it," Jeannette said.

"His old age would have been a better use."

That night, after the lights had been turned off in the room, Stephen said, "I hope you're right about the dream business, that Jean Marie really is you. My father believed you lived in people's memories and in your children. I want him to have more than that."

Chapter Twelve

Jean Marie, Sophie, and Mrs. Hastings sat in the waiting room at the emergency ward of the hospital. A doctor came from behind the swinging doors, looked at his clipboard, and called out, "Sophie Wilmslow?"

"That's me," Sophie said as she stood up.

The doctor joined them. He said, "Your mother's going to be fine. She'll be out as soon as she finishes talking to the police."

"How badly is Mrs. Wilmslow hurt?" Mrs. Hastings asked.

"She broke her collar bone when she was thrown against the car. Facial bruising, some bruising to the upper body. The man attacked her with his fists. No weapon was involved."

The doctor smiled, nodded, and moved on, clipboard in hand. "Theresa Valdez?" Jean Marie heard him call.

They sat back down and continued waiting.

I wonder what Jeannette would think of this hospital, how it compares to hers, Jean Marie thought.

"There's Mom," Sophie said.

Mrs. Wilmslow came into the waiting room with a policewoman. *Officer Reynolds,* Jean Marie realized, surprised.

Officer Reynolds came with Mrs. Wilmslow to join them.

"Hello, Sophie, Jean Marie," she said.

Sophie said, "Mrs. Hastings, this is Officer Reynolds. She came to the school after Mr. Jenks was attacked."

"Would you like to change your testimony, Sophie?" Officer Reynolds said. "After what that man did to your mother, you don't want to protect him. If you're afraid, he's in jail now."

117

"I'm glad he's in jail. I hope he stays there. But I slept all night that night and don't remember anyone leaving the trailer."

Mrs. Wilmslow said, "How long can you keep him locked up?"

"We've opposed bail. He's still a suspect in the Jenks case, and the judge will probably agree to deny bail. He's in jail until his trial, a couple of weeks, depending on how heavy the court docket is. At his trial, well, he's got no prior convictions. He didn't use a weapon. He may get off with a fine, depending on the judge."

"He may be out in three weeks."

"He may. You can get a court order telling him to stay away from your home and not to approach you on the street."

The policewoman left and they followed her into the parking lot.

"I know Cory's in jail, but I still expect him to jump out," Mrs. Wilmslow said.

Mrs. Hastings said. "I think you and Sophie should spend the night with us, Helen."

"No, we'll be all right."

After they got into the car, Sophie asked, "What happened, Mom?"

"It was going well. I thought Cory understood he had to move this weekend. I'd always told him this was temporary. Saturday, I set up some appointments to look at apartments. We went, he didn't like any of them. Sunday, I said he could go to a motel. I started putting his stuff in his car. He followed me out."

"He lost his temper and went crazy?" Sophie asked.

"No, he was perfectly calm. That made it worse. He said I needed discipline then he threw me against the car and started punching me in the face. I started screaming. Mrs. Henderson called the police. They took Cory to jail and me to the hospital. I called you. That's it."

"Do you think he killed Mr. Jenks?"

"I don't see how he knew where Mr. Jenks lived. He had an argument with the man at 3:30. Somebody attacked Mr. Jenks at 2 a.m."

"How does he get money?" Mrs. Hastings asked.

"He's a good mechanic. He was on the stock car circuit. He worked for some of the big names in racing. He got into too many fights. No one will hire him permanently, but he still gets called in as a consultant, a specialist. If he's a crook, he doesn't need to be."

"Then the police aren't going to solve our problem," Sophie said.

"Not very likely," her mother answered. She sounded exhausted. "I think the only thing to do is leave town."

Sophie wasn't in school the next day. Jean Marie tried calling her, but her cell phone was turned off.

Jean Marie got home at four and tried calling again. There was still no answer.

After dinner, Jean Marie heard the doorbell ring. When she opened it, Sophie and her mother stood outside.

"We had to tell you goodbye," Mrs. Wilmslow said.

Jean Marie's mother came to the door. "Come in."

Jean Marie looked out and saw Sophie's mother's car was packed.

They came in and Jean Marie's mother made coffee. The four of them sat down at the kitchen table.

"We're leaving town," Mrs. Wilmslow said. "Cory won't let up. I saw him in jail this morning, and he just laughed. He said we belonged together, the only problem was Sophie. He suggested I put her up for adoption."

"The man's mad!"

"No, just obsessive." Mrs. Wilmslow drank her coffee. "I told the police I'd fly back for his trial. They've got my cell phone number when the trial date is set. After I went to the police station, I went home and packed. The manager of the trailer park said he'd manage selling the trailer. Mrs. Henderson's sister might be interested. I just got paid and I've got a credit card. I'll stay with friends until I get another job."

"Where are you going?"

"It's better if I don't tell you, Jean Marie. I'm sorry, so sorry, I got you involved in this."

"I'm going to call you on your birthday," Sophie said.

"We'll be here," Jean Marie said.

"Give us a call when you come back for the trial," Mrs. Hastings said.

Jean Marie and her mother stood in the door and watched them drive away.

***

Jeannette decided not to tell Stephen about December 14. He would be gone before then, and he didn't handle the future very well. She told him about Cory, and about Sophie's disappearance.

"The police ought to do something. That's their job."

Jeannette felt irritated. "Stephen, they arrested him. He's going to be tried. What else can they do? Jean Marie is scared. So is her mother. Cory is calling from jail. He says he's sure Jean Marie knows where Sophie is."

"You haven't been working with your crutches," Stephen said.

"I have."

"Not enough."

Stephen refused to use a wheelchair. He'd taken to visiting Franz and the other men in their ward.

Stephen was always determined, and he now seemed determined to make her work as hard as he did.

"You're leaving the hospital, too. In time for Christmas in Wales. Snow, Jeannie-beanie, snow."

"Snow and crutches. That does sound delightful, Stephen."

"Snow and a sled," Stephen said. "While I'm slogging away at chemistry, you'll be sliding down Welsh hills, tucked up with a rug, some nice Welsh lad to pull you up again. Cups of cocoa …yum, yum. You just need to exert yourself."

"How are the steps going?"

"Could be better. But I won't need to go up and down, much. I'm going to be working with my tutor, preparing for the Cambridge Entrance Exam in June."

"You'll come first. First of all of them that take the exam. I'll read about it in the newspapers. They always print the names of the top scholars."

"Jeannette," Stephen said, "I tease you about premonitions. You're going to laugh when I say this, but I think you should leave the hospital as soon as you can. I have a very bad feeling."

"You're right. I'm laughing. Premonitions are my business, not yours." Jeannette said. "Go see Franz. Climb the steps to the roof. I work every day, and Paul is pleased. Stop bullying me, Stephen."

Stephen left and Jeannette sank into her favorite daydream. It was the same daydream she had before Jean Marie and all that happened. Matron was her mother, Mr. Finkelstein was her father, and Stephen was her big brother. She laughed at herself. It had changed slightly. They all lived in Wales, with sheep and a dog. It had changed in other ways as well. Those people she pretended were her family had become her family, good as, at least. And her Nan was there, too. By the big fire in the Welsh farmhouse.

Jeannette, get off your lazy butt and start working to get out of that hospital!

Jean Marie. She'd blocked any contact for days. The girl was persistent.

Jean Marie, Matron is immovable. A rock. She says we're going December 20. That's when her leave begins. Just what do you expect me to do? She's not Mr. Finkelstein. She believes in things she can touch and feel. She won't be persuaded.

Jeannette could feel Jean Marie's frustration through space and time. The girl could be a real shrew.

Stephen will be gone. That's good enough. I can barely walk ten feet with the crutches.

The Reynolds woman, Jeannette. Tell her you want to go to some miserable little place and learn to make artificial flowers. She'll get you out of the hospital.

But I don't, Jean Marie. I don't want to make artificial flowers. I don't want to see that horrible woman again. You're afraid, like I am, that if I live you don't. I think it's very honorable of you to try to persuade me to go. I'm proud of you. I'm proud of me, as well. Whatever happens, it's all right.

Chapter Thirteen

It was Jean Marie's birthday.

Her mother said, "Are you sure you don't want to invite Dawn or some other friend over?"

"Dawn's not a friend," Jean Marie said. "She's somebody I have lunch with."

She had thought Dawn was a friend. When the business with Jeannette and Stephen began, she'd tried telling Dawn about it. Dawn thought it was interesting and talked about ghosts. Then she'd told everybody else and Jean Marie spent a month listening to jerks hum the theme song from the X-files. No, Dawn was not a friend.

Jeannette had been a friend. Jeannette was gone. The Dream was gone. She was glad she hadn't experienced the bombing. Dying once was quite enough. Jeannette had just disappeared. She hoped Jeannette hadn't been afraid.

She had to talk to someone, so she told her mother. Her mother was skeptical, but at least hadn't insisted she see a shrink. Her stepfather Tim, on the other hand, was a science fiction freak and he'd been fascinated. First, they'd Googled the names: they found Stephen Finkelstein, Professor, Cambridge University, Nobel Prize winner 1995. Maybe, her stepfather said, but maybe not, the same one. He suggested she look through the microfiches, to get independent validation for the dreams, when she'd found the picture of Stephen and Sister Kenny.

Tim was the one she'd talked to after she found the date the hospital would be bombed. He'd pointed out that changing the past could change the present: did she want to risk that? If she and Jeannette were connected, how would her life change?

Tim reminded her of Mr. Finkelstein. They had the same feel. She wished she could still contact Jeanette, who could tell Stephen.

Jean Marie's mother sat down in an old armchair that had been dragged into the kitchen from the TV room. Her mother was too big to sit at the table.

"Children may be wonderful," her mother said, "but pregnancy is not. No one that is not at least eight months pregnant has a right to complain about anything."

Tim came into the kitchen with the Houston Chronicle. He sat at the table and started reading.

"Do you know a Kylie Wilmslow, Jean Marie? She went to your school…" he asked

"Kylie Wilmslow… name sounds familiar. I think she was on the pep squad. I didn't know her, she was a couple of grades behind me."

"She and her mother died in a fire. Arson. The fire had been set after someone beat them to death with a baseball bat. The mother's boyfriend was arrested."

The doorbell rang. Tim answered the door. He came back into the room and handed Jean Marie a package, "For the Birthday Girl. A registered package from England. I signed for it."

There were two jeweler's boxes and two letters inside the package. She opened one of the letters.

Dear Jean Marie, she read,

Jeannette gave me your address; she wrote it down as I was leaving. She made me promise to write you on your fourteenth birthday. I found your mother's name in the Houston telephone directory. So, if changes have occurred because of our meddling with time, at least there is still a Hastings at this address. I think it's due to you that I lived. Mrs. Reynolds would have blocked my return to school until after the 14th of December. I always wanted to see you, and, of course, Sophie.

I have found no trace of Sophie. Jeannette said Sophie and her mother left Houston because of Cory. I hope they are safely hidden somewhere. Jeannette said Sophie promised to call you on your birthday. Please give her my love and tell her to call me if I can help her in any way. I have worried a great deal about Sophie. Please write and tell me she is all right.

I'm sending you and Sophie matching lockets with pictures of myself and Jeannette. I think of that time in the hospital, and it seems as if four of us were there. Our times have finally come together, and it would be very pleasant to hear from you.

With all my love, and all my good wishes for today and for always, for now and forever,

your friend,

Stephen Finkelstein

"Sophie? Who's Sophie?" Jean Marie asked, bewildered. "Maybe the second letter will explain."

Dear Jean Marie,

My Uncle Stephen died eight months ago. I promised him that I'd mail this to you, to be delivered on your birthday.

David Finkelstein

Jean Marie opened one of the jeweler's boxes. Inside, she found a locket with her name on it: Jean Marie. When she opened the locket, she saw a picture of the boy Stephen and the girl Jeannette. *They took them on the day Stephen left for school.*

She handed the letter to her mother and opened the other box. The locket was identical except for the engraved name: Sophie.

Her mother read, and asked, "But who is Sophie? And Cory?"

"Sophie, Sophia for wisdom," her stepfather said. "A good name for a new daughter, I think."

For a moment, Jean Marie almost remembered a small, dark girl.

125

Jean Marie began to cry and she did not know why.

Printed in Great Britain
by Amazon